THE EARTH MYSTERIES WORKBOOK

THE EARTH MYSTERIES WORKBOOK
A One Year Course in the Enchantment of the Land

John Michael Greer

AEON

First published in 2024 by
Aeon Books

Copyright © 2024 by John Michael Greer

The right of John Michael Greer to be identified as the author of this work has been asserted in accordance with §§ 77 and 78 of the Copyright Design and Patents Act 1988.

All rights reserved. No part of this publication may be reproduced, stored in a retrieval system, or transmitted, in any form or by any means, electronic, mechanical, photocopying, recording, or otherwise, without the prior written permission of the publisher.

British Library Cataloguing in Publication Data

A C.I.P. for this book is available from the British Library

ISBN-13: 978-1-80152-121-5

Typeset by Medlar Publishing Solutions Pvt Ltd, India

www.aeonbooks.co.uk

CONTENTS

INTRODUCTION ix

UNIT ONE: Preparations 1
  Lesson 1: What are earth mysteries? 3
  Lesson 2: The seen and the unseen 7
  Lesson 3: The disenchantment of the world 11
  Lesson 4: The reenchantment of the world 15
  Lesson 5: The inner senses 19
  Lesson 6: Developing the inner senses 23
  Lesson 7: Dowsing 27
  Lesson 8: Psychometry 31
  Lesson 9: Attuning to nature 35
  Lesson 10: Seasonal cycles 39
  Lesson 11: Natural philosophy 43
  Lesson 12: In search of mysteries 47

UNIT TWO: Sites 51
  Lesson 13: Overview of sites 53
  Lesson 14: The earth currents 57
  Lesson 15: The land as palimpsest 61

Lesson 16: Mounds and earthworks	65
Lesson 17: Megaliths	69
Lesson 18: Shrines, temples, and churches	73
Lesson 19: Alignments 1—Leys	77
Lesson 20: Alignments 2—Spirit roads	81
Lesson 21: Alignments 3—The earth and the heavens	85
Lesson 22: Relics out of place	89
Lesson 23: Landscape patterns	93
Lesson 24: The language of the land	97
UNIT THREE: Stories	**101**
Lesson 25: Overview of stories	103
Lesson 26: The historical landscape	107
Lesson 27: The mythic landscape	111
Lesson 28: Myths and archetypes	115
Lesson 29: The legendary landscape 1—Legends of the past	119
Lesson 30: The legendary landscape 2—Legends of the present	123
Lesson 31: Stories of beginnings	127
Lesson 32: Stories of mysterious places	131
Lesson 33: Stories of mysterious events	135
Lesson 34: Stories of the future	139
Lesson 35: Stories of the conventional wisdom	143
Lesson 36: The narrative landscape	147
UNIT FOUR: Phenomena	**151**
Lesson 37: Overview of phenomena	153
Lesson 38: The phantasmagoria factor	157
Lesson 39: Ghosts and hauntings	161
Lesson 40: Mysterious animals	165
Lesson 41: Mysterious hominids	169
Lesson 42: Impossible creatures	173
Lesson 43: Appearances and disappearances	177
Lesson 44: UFOs 1—Unraveling the confusion	181
Lesson 45: UFOs 2—Earth lights	185
Lesson 46: UFOs 3—The shamanic dimension	189
Lesson 47: Flaps and windows	193
Lesson 48: Between two worlds	197

FOUR SAMPLE EXPLORATIONS	201
Sample Exploration 1: The legend of William Blackstone	203
Sample Exploration 2: The Glocester dragon	209
Sample Exploration 3: The Newport Tower enigma	215
Sample Exploration 4: The lost city of Norumbega	223
APPENDIX: Instructions for practice	229
Seed thoughts	229
Questions for reflection	229
Discursive meditation	230
Scrying	235
BIBLIOGRAPHY	239
INDEX	245

INTRODUCTION

The land on which we walk is full of mysteries. Some of these mysteries are timeless and ubiquitous, inseparable from the wonder and puzzle of human existence, but others are rooted in particular eras of history and places on the earth's surface. In some spots, ancient structures built by forgotten peoples baffle today's orthodox archeologists and historians. In others, myths and legends have left their traces. In still others, witnesses have encountered strange phenomena in our time. All these puzzles, linked as they are with specific places on the land, belong to the field of study that has come to be known as earth mysteries research.

There are many good reasons to investigate earth mysteries. Some people are drawn to the study of strange places, stories, and phenomena by the wholesome attractions of ordinary curiosity. Others become convinced that the officially accepted narratives about history and reality are mistaken, and plunge into the study of earth mysteries in a quest for the truth about past and present. Still others have had a personal encounter with something that fails to fit within the modern consensus of what is real, and go in search of explanations that will help them make sense of a world that has turned out to be far stranger than they expected.

All these and others are valid reasons to go in search of earth mysteries. This book can accommodate all of them, but its focus is slightly different. As an instructional workbook for members of the Golden Section Fellowship, it presents the study of earth mysteries as a branch of occult study and a spiritual discipline.

Let's take these latter concepts one at a time. The word "occult" literally means "hidden." In the Renaissance, when a handful of daring intellectuals took up the study of surviving texts about magic, divination, and alternative spirituality from ancient Greek times, the term they used for their forbidden studies was *occulta philosophia*—the hidden philosophy. By the nineteenth century, phrases such as "occult philosophy" and "occult practice" had been combined into the convenient word "occultism." Occultists today, like their equivalents in past centuries, practice ritual, meditation, and similar disciplines to learn how to perceive hidden aspects of reality, and attune themselves to the great currents of spiritual power and wisdom that people in past civilizations called gods and goddesses.

The Golden Section Fellowship is one tradition of occult study and practice. It is not an organization in the normal sense of the term: it has no officers and no headquarters, and its members pay no dues. It consists of those people who work with a particular set of occult teachings and disciplines, which have been published in several of my previous books—*The Way of the Golden Section, The Occult Philosophy Workbook,* and *The Way of the Four Elements*. It descends from several earlier occult traditions, and the goal its members seek is the attainment of wisdom, revelation, and enlightenment.

Almost anything can be used as a vehicle for occult training. In the monasteries of Asia practically every imaginable human activity from flower arranging and sexual intercourse to garden design and martial arts has been put to work in the quest for enlightenment. In the Western world, while the pressures of dogmatic religion made experimentation less easy, the traditions of Freemasonry show that sacred geometry and architecture were once practiced as spiritual disciplines. Investigating earth mysteries is less exotic than some other activities that have been given a spiritual focus, but this field of study also has a special relevance to the work of the Golden Section Fellowship.

To begin with, the sites, stories, and strange phenomena central to earth mysteries research are all places where the Seen and the Unseen come close together. Whether you're visiting a stone circle, chasing down variant forms of a half-forgotten legend, gathering data on sightings of a mysterious creature, or encountering some anomalous event yourself, your study of earth mysteries brings you directly or indirectly in contact with the human experience of the unknown. That experience is at the root of occultism, and it helps guide our quest for wisdom, revelation, and enlightenment. It is through such experiences that we can glimpse certain aspects of the hidden side of the universe.

Occult study and earth mysteries research also share an attitude toward the past that challenges the easy assumptions of contemporary life. Too many people nowadays believe that modern science has solved every problem that matters, and that the sacred knowledge of ancient times has to be wrong because it differs from the opinions of today's scientific bureaucrats. Occultists know better, because their studies and practices bring them into contact with sources of life, meaning, and power for which modern materialist ideologies make no place. Earth mysteries researchers know better, too, because their work constantly confronts them with enigmas that today's fashionable notions of reality and truth cannot explain.

Occultists and earth mysteries researchers both know that people in past ages knew much more about the subtle and spiritual dimensions of the land than we know today. They recognize that the ancients knew how to weave enchantments into the land, in ways that made it easier for human beings to live in harmony with other living things and with the greater cycles of nature. In recent centuries, much of that knowledge has been lost—but it can still be regained. The quest to understand and restore the ancient enchantments of the land is important to many occultists today, and it plays a special role in the work of the Golden Section Fellowship. By pursuing earth mysteries research, members of the Fellowship can train their minds and spirits, while contributing to this quest.

Working with the course

As the subtitle of this book makes clear, the material in the pages that follow is meant to be worked through over the course of one year. There are forty-eight lessons, each of which is meant to provide raw material for thought, study, and meditation for one week. Each lesson's Orientation section is divided into seven numbered paragraphs, and each of these should be used as a source of themes for a daily meditation during the week you spend on the lesson.

As explained later on, you should also plan on fitting in four personal explorations of earth mysteries into the year you spend on this book. Those explorations may be done at any point in your studies; four sample explorations given after the forty-eight lessons will give you some idea of what to look for and how to go about it. Each of these explorations should provide you with material for a week of meditation, completing the cycle of the year; you may carry out these meditations at any point in your studies, too.

If at all possible, you should plan on carrying out your investigations in the area in which you yourself live. One bad habit into which many earth mysteries researchers have fallen over the last century or so is that of thinking that only certain special locations on the earth's surface are worth bothering to study. It is of course true that some places have more ancient sacred sites, more local legends, or more unexplained phenomena than others, but there is no place on earth where the Unseen does not show itself now and then through the landscape in one way or another. It also happens far more often than not that close attention to a seemingly prosaic region will turn up plenty of neglected sites and long-forgotten collections of lore.

The available information on earth mysteries is so vast that only the briefest of overviews will fit into a single volume. This book is intended to give such an overview, oriented toward the specific aspects of earth mysteries that are of interest to occultists, but it cannot be complete. To build on that overview, you will need to read other books, articles, and websites. Since every part of the world has its own earth mysteries and no two places have exactly the same mix, your choice of sources to study will likely be unique to you. The bibliography at the end of this book contains a selection of classic books on earth mysteries, but there are many other written sources you may choose to explore as you pursue your explorations.

Books alone, however, are not enough. What trackers call "dirt time"—that is, time spent in the field, pursuing earth mysteries on the land itself—is also essential. You can learn a certain amount about earth mysteries inside a library or on the internet, but there are also things about them that can only be learned by going to mysterious sites, the settings of legends and stories, and the locations where strange phenomena have occurred. Only by combining these two paths of scholarship and fieldwork can you pursue the study of earth mysteries in earnest.

The most important resource you will need alongside this book is therefore one that you will create yourself. No two regions anywhere on earth have the same legends, traditions, stories, strange experiences, mysterious phenomena, and ancient relics associated with them. If you want to take your study of earth mysteries past the realm of abstract notions, or pleasant daydreams about places you have never been, you will need to gather information about the landscape in which you pursue your studies. The lessons ahead will help you get started collecting your local earth mysteries lore. You may be doing your earth mysteries research in a place where students of the earth mysteries have already built up a great deal of lore that you can use, you may pursue your work in a place where all you have to go on are a few books of folklore and a scattering of eccentric websites, or you may be in a place that falls somewhere between these two extremes. No matter which of these is true for you, the instructions that follow will teach you how to assemble enough material to work with.

A word of acknowledgment

I came of age in the middle of the occult revival of the late twentieth century, and earth mysteries research had a significant presence among the innovative ideas and colorful publications of that heady time. Two works in particular had a significant influence on my understanding of earth mysteries. The first was John Michell's *The View Over Atlantis*, a visionary work of landscape mysticism that revolutionized the field of earth mysteries from its first publication in 1969. The American paperback edition of 1972, with its vivid Roger Dean cover art, was my introduction to the field of earth mysteries; despite certain errors of detail, it remains an enduring source of inspiration to me.

The same is true of another, much less widely circulated work, the Ovate Grade correspondence course written by Philip Carr-Gomm and issued by the Order of Bards Ovates and Druids (OBOD) in the mid-1980s, which I studied in 1996 and 1997. Like most correspondence courses in the alternative spirituality scene, it covered a great many subjects, and it played a significant role in my inner development, but the theme that had the strongest influence on me was the way that it wove together the study of megalithic sacred sites with a living contemporary nature spirituality. That was my introduction to the concept that earth mysteries research can be pursued as a spiritual discipline.

I have drawn on a great many sources in the pages that follow. Readers familiar with either or both of the works just named, however, will notice certain echoes in this book. Those are quite deliberate, and are included in a spirit of homage.

UNIT ONE

PREPARATIONS

LESSON 1

What are earth mysteries?

Seed thought

"The green earth, say you? That is a mighty matter of legend, though you tread it under the light of day!"
—J. R. R. Tolkien, *The Two Towers*

Orientation

1. Scattered across the landscape of the planet, sometimes famous, more often forgotten, are places that differ in subtle ways from the countryside that surrounds them. A magic presence, hard to define but just as hard to ignore, hovers about these places. In some cases that presence was marked by ancient peoples, who shaped earthen mounds, raised standing stones, built temples, or in some other enduring way indicated the location as sacred. Other places were marked in ways that did not survive the centuries, or were left entirely untouched.
2. Every part of the world has such places. The history of different countries, however, has left behind very different traces of the sacred sites known to ancient peoples. Where a region has been settled by the same ethnic group for a very long time, much may still be

remembered about the sacred places of the land. Where the former inhabitants were dispossessed or died out in the last few centuries, by contrast, very little information may be preserved—and the heirs of the former inhabitants, if any survive, may not be interested in passing on what they know to the heirs of those who displaced them. Yet the magic presence remains, and can be sensed by those who develop the necessary skills.

3. Until the coming of modern times, the field of study now called "earth mysteries" was an ordinary part of life for rural people all over the world. Beginning in the seventeenth century, however, scholars in Britain, Germany, and a few other places began to recognize that the old rural knowledge of sacred spaces was dying out, and started collecting what they could. From those early efforts several different fields of study were born, including respectable branches of scholarship such as archeology and folklore studies.

4. Earth mysteries studies are not a respectable branch of scholarship. For reasons we will be exploring in later lessons, the intellectual mainstream of the modern world rejects any field of study that verges on the magical and the mystical. Mainstream scholars still like to put angry denunciations of such things into their books and lectures. Those who understand the power and meaning of the earth's sacred places laugh and proceed with their work, knowing that the scholars who do this have never studied the subjects they criticize so ignorantly.

5. What subjects come under the heading of earth mysteries? In the broadest sense, everything that might help cast light on the sacred places of the land can be included in this field. More specifically, however, earth mysteries studies center on three broad categories of information, which can be summarized as sites, stories, and phenomena. Sites include all the traces left in the earth by the practices of past peoples, such as the earthen mounds and standing stones mentioned earlier. Stories include myths, legends, folktales, and traditions that tell about the unusual properties of places. Phenomena include all unusual experiences that have been reported by witnesses in particular places.

6. Sites, stories, and phenomena are not evenly spread across the earth's surface. Some places have a substantial collection of things fitting one, two, or three of these categories. Others have none of them. This is why it makes sense to speak of some localities as being

sacred places, as distinct from others that are less sacred. As you collect information on the sites, stories, and phenomena in the region or regions that interest you, you may begin to grasp patterns that will guide you toward a clearer sense of the magic presence in the landscape.
7. That presence, however, remains at least a little elusive even to the most skilled student of earth mysteries. Compared to the ancients, we know very, very little about the subtle dimensions of the landscape. Though significant steps have been taken in recent decades by researchers into earth mysteries, the achievements so far are small in comparison to the work that remains to be done. One implication of this is that no matter who you are, and no matter where you happen to be, you can make important contributions to the quest.

Practical work

Before you begin collecting lore about the area you intend to study, stop and write down everything you already know about the subject of sites, stories, and phenomena in that area. If you know of ancient or mysterious sites in the region, note that down. If you know of local legends, folktales, and stories, note those down, and if you know of strange phenomena that have been sighted nearby, add those to the collection. Your list may be short or it may be long—that doesn't matter. By remembering whatever you know and writing it down, you begin the process of orienting your mind to the work ahead.

Question for reflection

What makes a feature of the landscape mysterious, and sets it apart from less mysterious places?

LESSON 2

The seen and the unseen

Seed thought

The instrument of all human enlightenment is an educated mind illuminated by revelation.
—John Michell, *The View Over Atlantis*

Orientation

1. To make sense of earth mysteries, it's necessary to start out from a point of view that the mainstream culture of our time rejects out of hand. Scientific and intellectual authorities these days like to insist that everything real is made of physical matter and energy, and that nothing other than these can possibly exist. That rigidly held belief—the dogma of materialism, as we can call it—underlies the entire worldview of the modern industrial world, and is responsible for many of the problems we face as individuals, communities, and societies today.
2. Occultists, by contrast, know that the universe of matter and energy is only a small portion of a much vaster cosmos. The basic elements of occult theory include an outline of this vaster cosmos, and much

of occult practice consists of exercises that teach students to pay attention to their inner senses and experience more of the cosmos than a narrow focus on matter and energy will allow.* By combining these studies and practices with explorations into earth mysteries, it becomes much easier to make sense of the subtle dimensions of the land.

3. Occult teachings include various descriptions of the nonmaterial dimensions of the cosmos. Just as a highway map and a topographic map include different symbols and highlight different parts of the landscape, the descriptions in occult literature vary because different schools and teachers focus on different aspects of the hidden side of existence. Fortunately, most work with earth mysteries can get by with a very simple way of making sense of the cosmos. We can set out that model of existence by dividing the world around us into two broad categories, which we can call the Seen and the Unseen.

4. You experience these two sides of existence every time you turn your attention to your own body. If you look at your hand, for example, the Seen consists of the material hand, with its palm and back and fingers, its skin and muscles and bones, which you experience with your outer senses. The Unseen consists of the will that enables you to move the hand, the sensorium that allows you to feel the hand, and the consciousness that moves through both; you experience these with your inner senses. The Seen and the Unseen are both constantly present in your hand and in every other part of yourself. You experience yourself in this twofold way at every moment, in everything you do.

5. One central principle of occultism is that this same twofold reality is present in everything else in the world, to one degree or another. Most of us recognize that animals have an unseen dimension of life, consciousness, and magic, just as we do. Some of us realize that the same thing is true of plants, even though the consciousness of plants is very different from ours. The occultist knows that it is true of everything. Stone, water, wind, sunlight, and even the apparent void of outer space are also full of life, consciousness, and magic, and we can perceive these things with our inner senses if we simply learn how.

---

*In the training program of the Golden Section Fellowship, *The Occult Philosophy Workbook* covers the basics of theory, and *The Way of the Golden Section* covers the essentials of practice.

Even the manufactured products that come out of our factories have their own unseen side, though the life, consciousness, and magic in them is very faint. In all things, the Seen and the Unseen are equally present.

6. Understand this and you have grasped the essential point in making sense of earth mysteries. The sites, stories, and phenomena that make up earth mysteries all involve places, times, and events in which the barrier between the Seen and the Unseen grows thin, and human beings can perceive the larger reality that lies behind the material world. That larger reality is always present, and those who have the necessary skills can always access it, but it is easier to reach in certain circumstances, and in those circumstances it sometimes shows itself even to those who have not yet learned the necessary skills.

7. The lesson to be drawn from this last point is that the Unseen is not wholly passive. It does not necessarily sit there waiting for some human being to do something about it. The seed thought for this lesson hints at how this lesson may be used. Students of earth mysteries, or of any other field of study, need to learn as much as possible about the subject they study, so that they know at least the outlines of what to look for and how to look for it, and so that they can respond intelligently to what they encounter. All this, however, is preparation for those moments when the Unseen reveals itself to the trained and attentive mind, and some long-hidden secret of the land becomes visible once more.

Practical work

As you go about your daily activities, make an effort to think about the presence of the Unseen in the world around you. Instead of treating the world as a lump of dead matter, treat it as something alive and conscious, which is capable of responding to your thoughts and actions. See what differences this makes in the way you relate to the world around you.

Question for reflection

How does the Unseen relate to the landscapes you experience around you?

LESSON 3

The disenchantment of the world

Seed thought

Two diametrically opposed worldviews are represented here—the ancient holistic continuum in which each part is related and responsible to each other, and the particular approach of the modern age, in which items can be isolated from the world and used without concern for the possible consequences. But "The world is a holy vessel," says the Tao Te Ching, "let him who would tamper with it, beware."
—Nigel Pennick, *The Ancient Science of Geomancy*

Orientation

1. More than a century ago the sociologist Max Weber proposed "the disenchantment of the world" as one of the most important features of modern life. In earlier times, he noted, most people experienced the world of nature as a realm full of life, consciousness, and magic, in which gods and spirits made their presence felt and human beings had to walk carefully. This was not simply a matter of belief or opinion. People actually experienced the world as living,

conscious, and magical. Many people today still experience the world this way.
2. For most people in the industrial world, however, the coming of modern times resulted in the dissolution of this enchanted state, so that they perceived the world as dead matter without life, consciousness, or magic. Once again, this was not simply a matter of belief or opinion. Most people in industrial nations stopped experiencing the life, consciousness, and magic in the world. Their state of disenchantment remains fixed in place for most people in these countries today. Disenchantment defines what these people experience when they encounter the world, and it also defines what can be discussed in public in our disenchanted society.
3. In eras of enchantment, people grow up learning to perceive the world through inner and outer senses together, so that the Seen and the Unseen flow together into a world made whole. In an era of disenchantment, by contrast, people grow up thinking that only the messages of the outer senses are real, and are taught to treat the inner senses as unreal and irrelevant. When disenchantment reigns, most people stop paying attention to what their inner senses tell them about the world. The decision to disregard the messages of the inner senses is what produces the disenchanted experience of reality, the sense that the world is mere dead matter.
4. In a time of disenchantment, most people believe that the disenchanted world is reality as it actually is, and insist that the enchanted world is a product of fantasy. Popular as this belief is in our disenchanted age, it is fundamentally mistaken. The secret of disenchantment is that it is also a product of the human mind and imagination. It is a condition of consciousness, not a reality out there in the world. People have to be taught from childhood on to imagine the world as mere dead matter, and that lesson has to be reinforced over and over again to make it stick.
5. Many of us can remember how, during our own childhoods, we were bullied, humiliated, and pressured into denying our own awareness of enchantment in the world. It can be helpful in understanding the experiences of enchantment and disenchantment to think back to your own childhood and remember times when the world seemed more alive, conscious, and magical than it seems to you today. It can also be helpful to recall times when you were mocked or punished for experiencing the world in an enchanted rather than a disenchanted mode.

6. Disenchantment is thus a choice we make as individuals and as a society. It is not a reality outside us. Enchantment is also a choice we can make as individuals and as a society. At present our society is deeply committed to disenchantment, and so the choice to experience the world as enchanted requires you to be willing to challenge some of the most basic assumptions taught by parents and teachers and promoted by authorities and the media. If you wish to reawaken your awareness of the enchanted world, you can expect pushback from many of the people you know and from the entirety of our collective culture.
7. Difficult as it is, the act of reawakening to enchantment in the world is a tremendous necessity for individual growth, and also for collective survival. It is because so many of us have fallen into the disenchanted world that we ourselves have become less alive, conscious, and magical than we can be. It is because so many of us have fallen into the disenchanted world that the world itself has been debased by human ignorance and greed. We cannot cope with the crisis of our age without first facing the wound in ourselves—the disenchantment we have allowed to take root within us—and restoring our awareness of the world's enchantment.

Practical work

During the week you spend on this lesson, explore your own experiences of enchantment and disenchantment. Were there times in your past when you were more attuned to your own inner senses and your experiences of the inner side of the world? Were there particular experiences you remember that made it difficult to keep that awareness? If you feel this would be helpful, write out an account of how your experiences of enchantment and disenchantment have changed over the course of your life.

Question for reflection

What parts of your everyday experience feel furthest from enchantment?

LESSON 4

The reenchantment of the world

Seed thought

It is magic, in every sense, that our civilization has lost, buried by the inadequacies of ignorant science and arrogant religion. And it is magic, in every sense, that our civilization needs, if it is to regain its sanity, its joy, its reason for being. An awareness of the magic of the earth has much to offer us in this respect; as we have seen, that magical worldview is of more value than those of science or religion when dealing with the whole of the reality of nature.

—Tom Graves, *Needles of Stone*

Orientation

1. In a strict sense, then, the world does not need to be reenchanted. It has never been without enchantment. Human beings, and in particular that minority of human beings who happen to live in the world's industrial societies, just need to recover the normal and natural ability to notice, experience, and work with the enchantments that have

been there all along. The task before us as individuals, cultures, and species is as simple as that.

2. "Simple," however, is not the same thing as "easy." The mask of disenchantment that we have collectively forced over the face of the world is held in place by potent emotional forces. It is because so many of us believe that the world is disenchanted, that it is no more than a mass of dead matter waiting for our species to do something with it, that our culture can pretend that humanity is the conqueror of nature, the master of the planet, the pinnacle and purpose of the entire evolutionary process. These outbursts of collective egomania, silly as they are, anchor the identity and sense of meaning of many people in the industrial world.

3. To accept that the world has always been enchanted—that it has always been full of life, consciousness, and magic, but some members of our species simply convinced themselves otherwise—is to have to let go of certain very deeply held beliefs. It requires us to recognize that we depend on the world, but the world does not depend on us; that the world was here long before we evolved and will still be here long after we are gone; that our hopes, our dreams, our beliefs, and our very existence matter to us, and to each other, but the world has its own concerns and does not pay attention to ours.

4. These recognitions can be very challenging for people raised in the cultures of the modern industrial world. This is one of the central reasons why earth mysteries are rejected by the scientific and cultural mainstream in the present day. To accept that the world is full of life and consciousness and magic, that ancient peoples knew more about these things than we do, and that they maintained constructive relations with the Unseen, threatens the foundations of the modern worldview. Yet the challenges involved in embracing the reality of enchantment are more than balanced by the benefits gained by doing so.

5. The disenchanted state is not a healthy one. It is physically unhealthy, since people under the spell of disenchantment no longer have the benefit of communion with the world through their inner senses, and cannot guide their relationships with the world, with each other, and with themselves by that means; ill health results from this lack of inner guidance. It is also emotionally and psychologically unhealthy. The tremendous burden of alienation and isolation that creates so much misery in today's world is entirely a product of disenchantment,

driven by the sense of a terrible void separating each of us from each other and the world.

6. This is why, as this lesson's seed thought suggests, the rediscovery of magic is so crucial a step in the healing of ourselves and our world. Our present societies are well stocked with technological trinkets and distractions, but very poorly supplied with such basic human requirements as wisdom and joy. To break through the illusion of disenchantment and reestablish a relationship with the enchantments of the world is to make a significant contribution to the healing of the world.

7. Earth mysteries research is only one of many ways to engage in this work. Yet it has certain significant benefits not necessarily shared by other approaches. To spend time in those places where a magic presence still lingers can make it much easier to shake off the spell of disenchantment. To study the secrets of the land can sometimes reveal some of the secrets of ancient enchantment. Approach these tasks with the trained mind and understanding of the practicing occultist and the doors to enchantment open readily before you.

Practical work

Building on the practical work you did for last week's lesson, reflect on those places that have been special to you during your life—the places where you felt more alive, joyous, and connected with the world. Think about what made those places different from other places you have been. If you have the chance, visit one of those special places and pay close attention to its effects on your thoughts and feelings.

Question for reflection

What parts of your everyday experience seem closest to the enchanted reality discussed in this lesson?

LESSON 5

The inner senses

Seed thought

Esoteric science begins where exoteric science ends. The latter derives its knowledge from observation of phenomena; the former works by intuitive methods.
—Dion Fortune, *Esoteric Orders and Their Work*

Orientation

1. As you prepare yourself for the training that will introduce you to earth mysteries research, it is crucial to remember that the Seen and the Unseen are not two separate worlds. Rather, they are two ways of experiencing the same world. The places we encounter with our outer senses are the same places we encounter with our inner senses. This has important consequences for the work ahead of you.
2. We perceive the Seen through our ordinary physical senses of sight, hearing, touch, scent, and taste, and we can supplement that with reports by other people who describe what they have perceived with their physical senses. We perceive the Unseen through a set of inner senses that are poorly understood and poorly appreciated in modern

industrial society. Every one of us has those senses, and every one of us knew how to use them before the pressures of society and schooling convinced most of us to ignore our own perceptions.

3. We experience our inner senses through that collection of mental activities we call the imagination. Please note that this does not mean that the inner senses are "imaginary," in the debased modern sense of that word! The human imagination is a much more complex thing than most people nowadays realize. Unquestionably, you can make up things with your imagination, and those things can be very vivid to you. At the same time, not everything you imagine is made by you.

4. If you clear your mind and allow images and ideas to rise up spontaneously in your mind's eye, you will find with practice that some of what appears does not come from your own thoughts, ideas, and memories. Among the things that can appear in this way are perceptions from your inner senses. With regular practice you can learn to tell the difference between the messages of your inner senses and the other things that appear in imagination, and begin to draw on your own intuitive insights in this way.

5. The fact that you are looking at the same world through two different sets of senses allows you to check the perceptions of each one against the other. Neither your outer nor your inner senses are infallible. Most people, especially when they begin training their inner senses, find that their outer senses tend to be the more accurate source of data, but when your perceptions differ it is always worth considering the possibility that this one time, the inner senses may be keener and bring you more accurate information.

6. This same principle applies when you check your own perceptions, inner and outer, against the perceptions of other people, whether you learn those from the people themselves or read about them during your research into the sites, stories, and phenomena in your region. More often than not, historians, archeologists, and others who use the outer senses to research the landscape will give you more accurate information than visionaries, mystics, and dreamers—but "more often than not" does not mean "always." Historians and archeologists have their biases and their rigid dogmas, and do not always have the common sense to discard these when the evidence challenges them. Visionaries, mystics, and dreamers are sometimes right.

7. Thus your work as a student of earth mysteries will require you to maintain a careful balance between the evidence from the Seen and the evidence from the Unseen, and between a healthy skepticism that asks necessary questions about unproven claims and a willingness to consider the possibility that the conventional wisdom may be wrong. As a later lesson will discuss in more detail, it is very often necessary to suspend judgment, to hold several conflicting ideas in your mind at the same time, and wait for further evidence before making up your mind. This is much more helpful than rushing to judgment in advance of the facts.

Practical work

During the week you spend on this lesson, make time to work with the process of clearing your mind and letting images rise up in your imagination. The technique of scrying introduced in *The Way of the Golden Section*, and in many other books on occult practice, is a systematized method of doing this. For this week's work, however, set aside the formal method and explore a more basic method. Simply sit down, clear your mind of thoughts as far as you can, and let images rise spontaneously into your awareness. If you have trouble getting anything to appear, imagine a door, then imagine yourself opening the door and see what is on the other side. Spend a few minutes doing this each day.

Question for reflection

When you think of your own experience of imagination, what memories and feelings come to the surface?

LESSON 6

Developing the inner senses

Seed thought

Therefore the first step in the pursuit of practical occultism is to train the mind, for only a very small proportion of occult work is concerned with phenomena perceived by the physical senses—it depends on the possession of some degree of psychic sensitivity for its appreciation. Yet psychism is really only hyper-sensitivity, and all of us are sensitive to a point, perhaps more so than we realize.
—Gareth Knight, *Dion Fortune's Rites of Isis and of Pan*

Orientation

1. The training offered by any school of occultism includes, among other things, an education in the use of the inner senses. The specific training provided in the Golden Section Fellowship is no exception to this rule. Discursive meditation, the core practice of the Fellowship, has many benefits, but one of them is that it clears away mental obstacles that interfere with our ability to perceive the messages of the inner senses. Scrying, another practice taught in the Fellowship

as an adjunct to meditation, focuses even more directly on learning how to pay attention to the inner senses.

2. In most systems of occult training, including the one taught in *The Way of the Golden Section* and its sequels, meditation and scrying are used to explore the meanings of traditional occult symbols, texts, and teachings. This is essential for the development of intuitive skills, and some degree of practice with such methods should be completed before applying the same skills to the study of earth mysteries. In any form of education, it helps to practice on what is already known before venturing into the unknown!

3. When you begin your own investigations into the sites, stories, and phenomena in your area, however, you should be prepared to apply the tools of discursive meditation and scrying to whatever you discover. These are important ways of engaging your inner senses and interacting with the world of the Unseen where it impinges on the land where you live. Treat the earth mysteries of your area as though they were occult symbols, texts, and teachings, and you will find that it is possible to learn a great deal from them.

4. Many students find that it works best to establish an alternating rhythm in these studies. Begin by finding out everything you can about a site, a story, or a phenomenon using your outer senses and such sources of information as books, websites, and eyewitness testimony. Once you have some sense of the outer aspect of what you are studying, move to the inner aspect and see what you can find out through meditation, scrying, and other occult methods. With whatever insights you have attained by those means, return to the outer world and see how your insights measure up to the evidence of the senses and recorded facts, and proceed from there.

5. If you have the opportunity to do so, it is worth making time to practice meditation and scrying at or near the site you are studying, or the place where a story is located or a phenomenon has been sighted. One of the things you will learn as you pursue these studies is that each place has its own distinctive influence, and attending to those influences using the tools of the practicing occultist is an effective way to learn more about it. It has happened tolerably often that occultists meditating in the place where a phenomenon has been seen find the phenomenon itself appearing in front of them.

6. It may not be possible for you to sit down in some corner of a place of interest and spend some time meditating. You will find that with

practice, locating yourself in the place in your imagination is nearly as effective. Many students find it best to imagine themselves journeying to the place by whatever means seem most appropriate. Once you arrive there, imagine the scene as vividly as you can, not just with the visual imagination but with every imaginary sense. What sounds do you hear? What scents are on the wind? What textures do you feel as you find a place to sit and begin your work?

7. It is usually best not to discuss these experiences with anyone else. At most you may want to share them with another person who is engaged in the same work as you. Partly this is because most people these days are still committed to the myth of disenchantment, and will not respond well if you challenge that myth in their presence. Partly this is because talking about your experiences is a good way to get your ego wrapped up in this or that belief about them, and that can be embarrassing when, as usually happens, later experiences cause you to reconsider your opinions. Yet there is a deeper level. As an occult adage has it, "strength is in silence." To talk freely about your experiences is to disempower them. To keep them private is to help them retain their transformative power.

Practical work

If you can manage it during the week you spend on this lesson, arrange to meditate at least once outdoors. If you can do this at a sacred site in your area, that's best, but if this isn't an option, any outdoor place will do. Whether you can do this or not, at least once during the week, travel in imagination to the outdoor place (if you were able to meditate there) or to some outdoor place, and meditate there. Take detailed notes on your experience.

Question for reflection

How do your experiences in meditation differ from what you experience in other ways?

LESSON 7

Dowsing

Seed thought

Dowsing is a skill, the basics of which anyone can learn with a little practice and awareness; but the problem is that the reliability of the results depends on the skill and experience of the dowser, among many other factors. There are plenty of inexperienced and over-confident amateur dowsers about, so perhaps the archaeologists are not being too evasive when they conceal the use of dowsing, as was the case at Cadbury-Camelot, under vague phrases in their reports, such as "probing with metal rods".

—Tom Graves, *Needles of Stone*

Orientation

1. The art of dowsing has been practiced since time immemorial in Europe and many other parts of the world, and was brought to the Americas by the earliest European settlers. Dowsers are most famous for being able to locate water sources, but books from the Middle Ages describe how miners relied on dowsing to find veins of ore,

and it is an open secret (as mentioned in the seed thought) that many archeologists today use dowsers to locate buried objects in archeological digs.

2. Dowsing remains far from respectable in today's society, however, because it relies on the inner senses. The dowser uses a device that is sensitive to subtle movements of the arms and hands—options include the traditional forked hazel stick, a pendulum, or a pair of L-shaped metal rods that can pivot freely in the hands. This allows unconscious muscle movements to become visible signs: for example, the forked hazel stick suddenly jerks up or down when the dowser walks across a water source. With practice, perceptions too faint to make their way directly into consciousness communicate through the dowsing process, allowing the dowser to sense the subtle signs of underground water, ore, and other things.

3. Because it relies on unconscious perceptions communicated through the body by indirect means, many people find that dowsing is somewhat more accurate than other ways of tapping into the inner senses. It is anything but foolproof, however. Inexperienced and unwary dowsers have made fools of themselves quite often by making grand claims on the basis of inadequately checked perceptions. This has been a particular problem in some parts of earth mysteries research. Some sense of the history behind this problem will help explain this.

4. Early in the twentieth century, dowsers and students of earth mysteries began to realize that they were perceiving different sides of a common reality. Dowsers who explored stone circles and other megalithic sites discovered apparent currents of energy that seemed to link one site to another, following the same routes as the leys that earth mysteries researchers were discovering at the same time. By the late twentieth century, as a result, dowsing became a common element of earth mysteries research. Many investigators in the earth mysteries field accordingly learned to dowse, cultivated relationships with skilled dowsers, or both.

5. Used intelligently in conjunction with other sources of data, dowsing has proved to be a very useful tool for making sense of the jumbled and fragmentary data of earth mysteries. Used unintelligently, without an adequate grasp of other sources of knowledge, dowsing has proved to be an unfailing source of misinformation and outright nonsense, so that some earth mysteries researchers these days want nothing to do with the dowser's art. In particular, insisting that you

have discovered a ley or a sacred site, when the only evidence for this claim is the reaction of your dowsing tools, will make more experienced researchers roll their eyes and walk away.
6. Dowsing can be learned from books, though many people find that learning it from an experienced practitioner is a better option. The essential element in effective dowsing training is checking your results against the evidence of the outer senses. Before you try to find sacred sites or trace leys across the countryside, see if you can find lost keys in your home, or locate something that another person has deliberately hidden for you to find. Once you can do these things reliably, then you can consider putting your skills to use in earth mysteries research.
7. Dowsing is not one of the disciplines assigned to initiates of the Golden Section Fellowship. However, it is entirely compatible with the work of the Fellowship, and with other branches of occult study and practice. It is up to you to decide whether you want to acquire the necessary tools, put in the necessary time and effort to become a competent dowser, and apply the resulting skills in your investigations into earth mysteries.

Practical work

During the week you spend on this lesson, look up dowsing using whatever sources of information you prefer to use for research; your local public library will likely have books on the subject, and of course the internet has plenty of information, though it tends to be of very uneven quality. Consider whether this is a skill you want to develop, and if so, look into sources of information and instruction in dowsing that are available to you.

Question for reflection

What thoughts and feelings come to mind when you consider the possibility of taking up the practice of dowsing?

LESSON 8

Psychometry

Seed thought

You must often have heard people say, when looking at some item of historical interest, "What a tale it could tell, if it could only speak." Those of us who have practical knowledge of what is popularly known as ESP know from our own experience that this saying is true. The historic article, indeed every article, not only has a tale to tell, but it is telling it constantly.
—W. E. Butler, *How to Read the Aura, Practice Psychometry, Telepathy and Clairvoyance*

Orientation

1. The word "psychometry" was coined in 1842 by Dr. Joseph Rodes Buchanan, a respected American physician and medical educator who learned this application of the inner senses through his own experiments. Under other names, however, it has been practiced since the most ancient times. Saints, shamans, and holy people around the world and throughout time have had the gift of coming into contact

with a physical object and reading from that object its history, and the personal experiences of those people connected with the object.
2. Of all the practical applications of the inner senses, psychometry is the easiest to learn. While the talent for psychometry varies from person to person like any other talent, most people can develop a basic level of skill in psychometry with a modest amount of training and practice. The most important ability the novice psychometrist needs to master in order to learn how to read mental and emotional impressions from an object is the ability to clear the mind and allow spontaneous images to rise—the same ability that is used in scrying and in many other branches of occult practice.
3. As with all the applications of the inner senses, however, psychometry is inexact, and subject to a variety of interfering factors. Classic psychometric training thus makes use of objects whose history is known, and which are presented to students who do not know what they are handling. The accuracy of their experiences can thus be checked in detail. Just as with dowsing, it is important to develop proven skill detecting known things before putting one's abilities to work ferreting out the unknown.
4. You will find that in earth mysteries research, and more broadly in psychometric practice, you will get better results if you can work with a physical object directly connected with the subject of your research, or better still, in a specific place connected with that subject. It is easier to get a clear reading if you can place your hands on one of the standing stones that compose a sacred site, or stand or sit on the ground where a strange phenomenon has been witnessed. Doing so from a distance is considerably more difficult.
5. Using psychometry at a distance has an even more serious drawback, because it is embarrassingly easy for the novice psychometrist to tap into impressions laid down by other minds as a result of mass media. Plenty of people who have tried to use psychic methods to get information about ancient Atlantis, for example, clearly picked up on the reactions of people in recent times whose emotions were stirred by watching a movie or read a novel about Atlantis. Since the drowning of Atlantis, according to Plato's account, occurred more than 11,000 years ago, its psychometric traces are much fainter than those laid down in recent decades by people watching movies about Atlantis on television!

6. Thus psychometry, like other applications of the inner senses, cannot be used all by itself. It must never be treated as infallible. Especially in the first few years you practice it, you can expect any accurate information you receive to be mixed up with a jumble of inaccuracies, some of them the product of your own mind, some the products of other human minds, and some from stranger sources. It takes practice and the application of common sense to sort through the results of psychometric investigation. Hints and glimpses received by psychometry, however, can be valuable if they are backed up by other sources of information.
7. Like dowsing, psychometry is not one of the disciplines assigned to initiates of the Golden Section Fellowship, but it is entirely compatible with the work of the Fellowship, and with most other branches of occult study and practice. Whether or not you choose to invest the necessary time and effort into studying and practicing psychometry, so that you can put it to work in earth mysteries research, is up to you.

Practical work

During the week you spend on this lesson, look up psychometry using whatever sources of information you prefer to use for research, and see what you can find out about methods of training. Consider whether this is a skill you want to develop, and if so, look into sources of information and instruction in psychometry that are available to you.

Question for reflection

What thoughts and feelings come to mind when you consider the possibility of taking up the practice of psychometry?

LESSON 9

Attuning to nature

Seed thought

He roamed, fished, hunted, searched for roots, lay in the grass or crouched in trees, sniffed, listened, imitated the voices of animals, kindled little fires and compared the shapes of the smoke clouds with the clouds in the sky, drenched his skin and hair with fog, rain, air, sun, or moonlight.
—Hermann Hesse, *The Glass Bead Game*

Orientation

1. The four previous lessons have focused on the development of the inner senses. The outer senses are also important in earth mysteries research. The keener your senses, and the more thoroughly you train them to pick up the messages brought to them by the natural world, the more successful you will be in making sense of sites, stories, and phenomena, the raw materials of earth mysteries studies.
2. This is partly because some things that look mysterious at first glance turn out to be much more prosaic if you pay close attention to them. Equally, mysterious phenomena can pass you by if you're not

familiar enough with the natural world to know when something is genuinely strange. It's difficult or impossible to recognize the presence of the supernatural if you do not yet have a good clear sense of what is natural. That sense is best developed by spending time in nature and attending to her moods and activities.

3. Yet there is a further dimension at work here. No great gap separates the Seen and the Unseen, the natural and the supernatural. To attend to nature, to learn to sense what she does and how she does it, sharpens and focuses the inner senses as well as the outer senses. Many people who spend much of their time in natural environments end up with an uncanny sense of what will happen, which draws on the inner and outer senses alike. That combined awareness is worth developing, and it can be learned in a simple and straightforward way.

4. The first and most crucial step in this mode of development is to spend some time outdoors every week, and if possible, every day. If nothing else, you can take a few minutes by an open window watching the sky and what living things you can see, but it is better if you can go into a park, a garden, a vacant lot abandoned to weeds, or any other place where there are plenty of living things and you can stand or sit beneath the open sky. Make this a regular practice. When you are doing it, focus your awareness on nature as intently as you would pay attention to the theme of a meditation.

5. Books, websites, and other sources of information about the natural world can be helpful as a resource in this work, but they can also interfere with the development of sensitivity to nature. If you find a guidebook to the trees of your region, for example, it can help to look up the trees in the area where you are spending time outdoors, so that you can learn something about their lives and their relationships to other living things. Never let that information distract you from paying close wordless attention to the trees you encounter. Treat it as a supplement to, not as a replacement for, direct personal experience.

6. The same rule applies to books about the birds and other living things of your region, the geology of the land beneath you, and the clouds and other weather phenomena above you. All these can be studied by way of books and websites, and so long as you don't let those get in the way of personal experience, this can be a very useful supplement to your studies. You may find it helpful to divide your time learning about nature into two sections, one spent paying

attention to nature, the other spent looking up details in books or websites and seeing how that information matches your own experience.
7. Knowledge of this kind has an advantage to the earth mysteries researcher that goes beyond the development of intuitive knowledge. Many times mysterious sites and phenomena are marked by unusual behavior in animals, unusual growth patterns in plants, and unusual forms in earth and stone. If you know the way the birds of your area behave, you will notice at once when they suddenly fall silent for no obvious reason; if you recognize the rocks of your region, an ancient standing stone brought from some distant place will stand out from its surroundings. Attuning yourself to nature thus gives you another way of sensing when and where the Unseen comes into contact with the Seen.

Practical work

During the week you spend on this lesson, begin spending more time outdoors. To accomplish anything, this practice needs to be kept up for a long time—it is not something you can pick up one week and set down the next. At least once a week, and preferably more often, arrange to spend time outdoors in various locations, paying attention to the plants, the earth, the sky, and anything else you encounter that was not put there by human beings. Keep notes in your earth mysteries journal, and you will be able to look back later and watch the growth of your awareness.

Question for reflection

How do you relate mentally, emotionally, and physically with the natural world around you?

LESSON 10

Seasonal cycles

Seed thought

The Arthurian myth clearly embodies the northern season cycle. The twelve knights are the heavenly star-signs whose flashing sword-dance induces fertility at the year's opening, frees the frozen waters for the coming of the spring.
—Ross Nichols, *An Examination of Creative Myth*

Orientation

1. Among the things you will quickly begin to perceive if you spend time outdoors are the powerful effects of seasonal cycles on living things. Across much of the earth's surface, seasonal cycles govern every phase of plant and animal life and drive the annual changes in weather. Learning to recognize these cycles is an important part of attuning yourself to nature, and will help you develop the broad intuitive perceptions and the specific awareness of changes in the natural order discussed in the previous lesson.
2. It will also help you understand the thoughts and traditions of those who lived in past eras. It can be hard for people today to grasp just

how important the seasons were before cheap fossil fuel energy transformed human life. The changing length of day means little to those who can simply turn on a light; central heating makes summer and winter less important than they once were; strawberries in December, a dream suited only for fairy tales in earlier times, are as close as the nearest grocery today. That the modern state of affairs may well turn out to be a temporary extravagance does not change its impact on our ways of thinking about the world.

3. In ancient times, by contrast, seasonal cycles defined the entire structure of human life. The hours of daylight, the length of the growing season, and the regular cycles of plant and animal life were realities that had to be kept in mind by everyone. As a result, these cycles are a constant factor in many of the things that earth mysteries researchers study.

4. Many sites, for example, are oriented toward specific positions of sunrise or sunset. Stonehenge, famously aligned on midsummer sunrise, is the most famous example, but plenty of less famous and less lavish structures from ancient times are similarly arranged. Such alignments are essential when knowing the proper times for planting and harvest, and for moving livestock out to upland pastures and back in to the lowlands; they were critical for human survival. They also tie into subtler and stranger cycles, of the sort studied by occultists today.

5. Stories, the second branch of earth mysteries studies, are also full of references to seasonal cycles. While the scholarship of an earlier age was mistaken in thinking that all myths everywhere have to do with the movements of the heavens, it is unquestionably true that many cycles of myth and legend relate to the cycles of the seasons, to the movements of sun, moon, planets, and stars, and to the life cycles of food plants and livestock. Understanding seasonal cycles will help you grasp the meanings of these stories and relate them to other aspects of the earth mysteries you investigate.

6. Phenomena can also be closely linked to seasonal cycles. Certain kinds of uncanny phenomena cluster so reliably at certain points in autumn in the temperate zones that festivals oriented toward the dead—Samhain, All Hallow's Eve, *Dia de los Muertos*, and others— collect around that time. Certain other times of the year have similar reputations in other cultures. As you investigate strange phenomena, pay attention to seasonal patterns and you will very often discover

unexpected clues to the nature and meaning of the mystery you are studying.
7. Modern industrial culture has an unhelpful habit of thinking of time solely as a *quantity*—so many minutes or days or years, all of them as interchangeable as machine parts. The ancient vision of time, shaped by the experience of seasonal cycles, recognized that each time also has its own *quality*, and that each minute or day or year is different from every other. From this recognition came ideas of fortunate and unfortunate days, favorable and unfavorable days of the lunar cycle, and much more, including the intricate systems of astrology evolved by Sumerian, Indian, Chinese, and Mesoamerican cultures millennia ago. As with dowsing and psychometry, whether you study any of these systems is up to you, but they can be valuable assets in making sense of earth mysteries from an occult perspective.

Practical work

As you continue spending time outdoors, look for indications of the changing seasons. Meanwhile, see how much information you can find about traditional seasonal practices in the region where you live. When were the important holidays, and what did they commemorate? When were crops planted, and when were they harvested? What other events marked the cycles of the seasons where you live? Learn as much as you can about this.

Question for reflection

What does the cycle of the seasons mean to you personally?

LESSON 11

Natural philosophy

Seed thought

Those, like Aubrey, by whom the great discoveries in any age are made, are always those who have prepared themselves for revelation by the cultivation of such interests as characterize the natural philosopher.

—John Michell, *The View Over Atlantis*

Orientation

1. One way to talk about the kind of awareness that you will need to cultivate as a student of earth mysteries is to reflect on a different form of awareness, the one cultivated by scientists in today's society. Scientists nowadays are specialists, focusing on some narrow sub-sub-subsection of a field of study, and they must restrict their studies to topics that will win the approval of their peers and the more tangible support of whoever pays for their research. They are rarely free to investigate whatever they wish or to follow the data wherever it leads.

2. Scientists are also expected to accept certain materialist dogmas. For example, the dogma that matter, energy, and empty space–time are the only things that actually exist, and the dogma that every physical event must have a physical cause, are required beliefs among scientists. Scientists who publicly disagree with these dogmas can expect to lose their funding, jobs, and reputations. Every decade or so, in fact, some formerly respectable scientist gets driven out of their field for the crime of discovering something he or she is not allowed to find.
3. This approach to understanding the world is however quite recent. Less than two centuries ago, the word "scientist" did not even exist—it was invented in the 1840s—and the word "science" referred to any field of organized knowledge, whether it conformed to the dogmas of materialism or not. Until that time, and for centuries before then, researchers into the secrets of nature had a different name and followed a different approach. They were called natural philosophers, and their way of investigating was more individualistic, more open, and more inclusive than the one that replaced it.
4. To natural philosophers, anything could be a subject of inquiry. John Aubrey, the natural philosopher mentioned in this week's seed thought, is a case in point. Aubrey was passionately interested in every kind of knowledge about English antiquity, whether or not it conformed to the dogmas or preconceptions of his time. That background enabled him to see what others missed—in a famous example, to visit the Wiltshire village of Avebury in 1648 and realize for the first time in modern history that the neglected standing stones around the village were part of a gigantic circular temple raised in the forgotten past.
5. The difference between science and natural philosophy can be neatly summed up in two words, one familiar, the other much less so. Science nowadays is governed by *consensus*: the common opinion of the entire scientific community determines the dogmas that scientists must believe, and the common opinion of each branch of science determines which research projects will get funding and which findings will be accepted by the community. Natural philosophy, by contrast, is governed by *dissensus*.* This is the principled avoidance of consensus, and encourages each natural philosopher to go his or her

---

*This term was coined by philosopher Ewa Ziarek, see Ziarek 2001 in the bibliography.

own way, following the data wherever it leads and pursuing research projects whether or not anyone else considers them worthwhile.
6. Embracing dissensus and going your own way in any field of studies involves certain risks. There is always the risk that the path you choose will turn out to be a dead end, and your life's work may consist of showing future students in the same field what not to do. There is the subtler risk of becoming emotionally committed to a theory, and trying to pile up evidence to support the theory rather than asking the hard questions that might disprove it. People pursuing modes of study governed by consensus also run these risks, but they can count on support and encouragement from others in the same field. Practitioners of dissensus have no such safety net. Their successes and failures are entirely their own.
7. The great advantage of natural philosophy, and of dissensus in general, is that they make it easier to get outside the rigid habits of thought that keep most inquiries into nature hobbled by current prejudices. An omnivorous interest in any branch of knowledge that might bear on a chosen subject, a willingness to ask questions that the conventional wisdom rules out of bounds and to accept the answers even if those contradict the approved beliefs of the time, and a freedom to cross the lines between disciplines and follow the data wherever it leads, transforms the quest for knowledge into a grand adventure.

Practical work

Take some time to reflect on the materialist dogmas mentioned earlier in this lesson. If you have already developed an interest in some part of earth mysteries research, reflect also on the officially established dogmas bearing on that field of study. Then consider whether the alternative views you know of also have dogmas, and reflect on those. Finally, assess your own beliefs. What are your personal dogmas? What beliefs about the universe would you consider true no matter what the evidence said?

Question for reflection

If you could study anything at all about the natural world, what would it be?

LESSON 12

In search of mysteries

Seed thought

In searching for the secrets of ancient enchantment we are in effect seeking the Grail, for the Grail legend is of a former enchantment, now broken, which will one day be restored. One day the lost Grail will be found again. It is a vessel which gives nourishment. It heals a sick people and transforms their disenchanted country, the wasteland, back into its natural, primeval character as the terrestrial paradise.

—John Michell and Christine Rhone, *Twelve-Tribe Nations and the Ancient Science of Enchanting the Landscape*

Orientation

1. To explore earth mysteries is to venture into a landscape of mysteries like the forest of Broceliande in the legends of King Arthur, where no signposts mark the way and anything might confront the questing knight. The secrets that guided the placement and function of ancient sacred sites were lost many centuries ago. The inner meanings of

myths and legends remain a puzzle despite many years of earnest labor by scholars and mystics. What lies behind the strange phenomena that confront startled witnesses all over the modern world is a mystery that still confounds even the most knowledgeable researcher.

2. We are far from the point at which any one student of earth mysteries can expect to gain a complete understanding of the whole picture. We cannot even be sure that everything currently assigned to the category of earth mysteries is a single picture, and not two or three (or more!) separate things that have been jumbled together as a result of our ignorance. What earth mysteries researchers have to work with at present is a grab bag of facts, reports, and rumors, many of which still need the most basic kinds of investigation.

3. Frustrating though they can be, the confusions and uncertainties of earth mysteries research are among the factors that make them useful in occult training. To be an occultist is to venture beyond the borders of the familiar, to deal with things most people consider nonexistent, and to pursue knowledge that was much better understood in the past. Earth mysteries embody all of these things, and provide a useful way of developing skill in working with the Unseen in its manifestations in the world around us. Approach your earth mysteries research as part of the process of becoming a more capable occultist and they will teach you much.

4. The perspectives of occultism also offer useful insights into earth mysteries and practical methods for exploring their subtle dimensions. As already noted, the inner senses are no more infallible than the outer senses, but they can provide insights of great value if they are used skillfully. The teachings of occult philosophy also provide a perspective from which many of the seemingly puzzling features of earth mysteries and unexplained phenomena make sense. Many earth mysteries are no mystery at all to those who know their way around occultism.

5. Be aware, however, that occult insights may not be welcome among students of earth mysteries who do not share the same background. It has happened tolerably often in recent history that clear explanations of baffling phenomena have been dismissed even by alternative thinkers because they were linked to occultism. Students of UFO lore may recall how the occult perspective on aerial apparitions, first presented by Meade Layne in the early days of the phenomenon and developed in great detail by John Keel and others in the 1960s and

1970s, was dismissed out of hand by those who insisted that UFOs could only be real if they were made of physical matter. The same dogmatic materialism hinders study in many other fields.
6. In studying any mysterious phenomenon, it is always worth considering the possibility that it has a purely material explanation, whether that explanation has to do with unfamiliar laws of nature, misunderstandings of well-known events, or human trickery and fraud. Assuming that any mysterious phenomenon must be reducible to a material cause, however, is just as unhelpful as assuming that any mysterious phenomenon must have a supernatural origin. Keep your mind open to both sets of possibilities and the chance of understanding increases sharply.
7. In a broader sense, this is true of everything that occultists study. We live in a cosmos in which the Seen and the Unseen, the world of physical matter and the worlds of subtle and spiritual forces, are in constant contact and just as constantly interpenetrate and influence one another. Learning to pay attention to both, to recognize the laws and limits of the material plane but at the same time to recognize the presence of spirit in matter, is to take an important step toward the wisdom, revelation, and enlightenment that students of occultism seek. It is also to approach earth mysteries in a way that can reveal their secrets.

Practical work

Review the twelve lessons of Unit One, and put some time into thinking about how you will approach the work of the units ahead. If you have decided to pursue training in dowsing, psychometry, or both, decide how you will fit the necessary work into your schedule of practices. If you have not already begun compiling data on the sites, stories, and phenomena in the area where you live, as described in the introduction, start doing this now. Get ready for the adventure ahead of you!

Question for reflection

What role do you see earth mysteries research having in your life at this time?

UNIT TWO

SITES

LESSON 13

Overview of sites

Seed thought

A stone wall, yes, or an aligned boulder, but what did the wall mean to those who built it? Where did it point and why? What did the boulder align with, and what lesson or story did it hold? What immortal thought or belief is framed in the ancient undertaking?

—Glenn Kreisberg, *Spirits in Stone*

Orientation

1. Ancient and mysterious sites are among the most obvious subjects for earth mysteries research. The entire field of earth mysteries began when a handful of researchers in Britain and Germany began paying attention to the mounds, standing stones, and other archaic sites in their own countries, and noticed strange things about them. The same focus remains in place in many parts of the world. This is understandable, since very little stirs the human imagination more forcefully than a puzzling ancient ruin. When was it made?

Who made it, and why? Such questions form the starting point of many quests.

2. Sites of interest to earth mysteries researchers are found all over the world. For every famous example, such as Stonehenge in England or Rhode Island's enigmatic Newport Tower, there are thousands of less famous locations of equal interest. Many of these are little known outside the earth mysteries community. New England, to cite only one example, has over 3000 megalithic sites of unknown origin and purpose, and yet it is relatively sparsely provided with such sites compared to upstate New York or the southern and central Appalachians.

3. One important point to keep in mind is that most human societies that lived before the beginning of the industrial age had a more pragmatic and open-minded attitude toward the Unseen than do most people today. Consider England, which has seen the rise and fall of so many societies over the ages. Medieval priests, Dark Age monks and hermits, Roman augurs, and Celtic Druids all understood the interpenetration of the Seen and the Unseen, and all the surviving evidence suggests that the astronomer-shamans of the megalithic age who laid out the stone circles and barrows had some similar vision of the cosmos.

4. Thus any site dating from before 1600 or so, provided that it had some connection to the spiritual realm, is worth considering as a possible focus for earth mysteries research. Where more than one ancient people left their traces behind, this can lead to considerable confusion, though it can also point up a site of particular importance: a location that was recognized as spiritually charged by the peoples of more than one culture and age will very often be a potent center of the influences of the Unseen.

5. The other two general categories of raw material for earth mysteries research, stories and phenomena, are also worth keeping in mind in the quest for mysterious sites. Many myths and legends are associated with specific places, the way that Mount Olympus in Greece became the anchor for the myths of the Greek gods and the Rhine valley in Germany became the setting for the legends of Siegfried and the golden treasure of the Nibelungs. Sometimes an old story can be a clue leading to a forgotten site; in other cases, a site remains enigmatic until some half-forgotten story offers clues to its original function and meaning.

OVERVIEW OF SITES   55

6. Phenomena are also very often closely associated with specific locations. These can be as exact as the spot along a lonely road where a phantom black dog has been seen at irregular intervals for the last 300 years or so, or as broad as the "windows" 200 miles across in which the mysterious aerial lights and shapes called UFOs tend to gather during periods of activity. As you collect information about phenomena in your area, keep track of any clue that suggests that they are connected to particular places or areas, and pay attention to these indications as you develop your sense of the local geography of the Unseen.
7. You can learn a great deal about sites from libraries and the internet, but nothing replaces personal experience of a place where uncanny forces show themselves in the world of everyday matter. Plan on visiting as many sites in your area as you reasonably can, alone or with people who won't be baffled or upset if you spend some time sitting still, using your inner senses to see what you can perceive. Far more often than not, nothing obviously paranormal will happen during such visits, but each visit to a place where the Unseen is awake will help develop your inner senses and assist your occult training generally.

Practical work

Sort through the material you have already gathered on earth mysteries in the area where you live, and identify as many ancient sites as you can. As you continue gathering information, keep a list of sites you might decide to investigate. When stories or phenomena are associated with specific places, include those places in your list as well. See if you can get a general sense of the geography of the Unseen in your area. Begin planning your first visit to at least one of the sites you have identified.

Question for reflection

When you think about ancient sites in the area you are studying, what thoughts and feelings come to mind?

LESSON 14

The earth currents

Seed thought

The spirit of the valley is eternal.
It is woman, the mother of all things.
It is like a veil that can scarcely be seen.
Rely on it. It will never fail you.

—Lao Tsu, *Tao Te Ching*

Orientation

1. To understand the role of sites in earth mysteries it is crucial to remember that the Unseen was present in the landscape long before the first human beings came on the scene. Most ancient sites of spiritual importance, in fact, were placed where they were because their builders could sense the hidden dimensions of the land and chose a place to build where nature already concentrated the subtle energies of the cosmos. Not all such places were marked by human structures even in ancient times, and many of the markings that were made have long since been erased by time and human ignorance. Other clues, however, can lead to them.

2. The most thoroughly developed system of understanding the natural flow of subtle energies in the earth is the Chinese system of *feng shui* (pronounced "fung shway"). While it has been popularized and debased in many modern Western works into a slightly exotic form of interior decorating, *feng shui* in its original form is a rich and complex system of understanding the presence of the Unseen in the landscape. Some students of earth mysteries have taken the time to study traditional *feng shui* in detail, while many others have learned the basic principles of the art.
3. Central to traditional *feng shui* is the concept of two currents that flow through the landscape, the two aspects or polarities of the life force. These are called poetically the blue dragon and the white tiger. The blue dragon, the yang or active current, flows along ridge lines and in high ground. The white tiger, the yin or receptive current, flows along the undulations of lower ground. Some landscapes are unbalanced in one direction, some in the other; some—for example, flat ground—have neither; where both are present, preferably in a balance of three-fifths yang and two-fifths yin, is the best place for a tomb, a temple, or any other structure that is meant to concentrate fortunate influences.
4. Both these currents naturally follow curves through the landscape, and where they coil around each other, their interaction brings good fortune. Straight lines, by contrast, are held by *feng shui* tradition to be dangerous. Depending on their location and direction, they can bring one of the two currents in excessive amounts, or drain one of the currents away, leaving a shortage. The harmful energy that moves along straight lines is called *sha*, and many *feng shui* texts refer to straight lines pointing directly to or from a site as "arrows of *sha*" which must be warded off like physical arrows.
5. Straight lines of any kind are therefore dangerous according to *feng shui* principles. They are not entirely forbidden, however. Even in imperial China, when *feng shui* governed the placement of every building, straight "spirit paths" were made to and from Imperial tombs to direct their influences in specific directions. The danger caused by "arrows of *sha*" is a matter of too-intense flows of the earth currents, and a skillful practitioner can put that high intensity to work in certain ways.
6. This is relevant to earth mysteries because the same principles were used in places very far from China. Many ancient stone circles and

earthen mounds in the British Isles, for example, are located exactly where a *feng shui* practitioner would place them, where the blue dragon and white tiger coil around each other beneficently. Similarly, the leys or straight alignments discovered by Alfred Watkins consistently did not pass over the old earth-walled forts of Neolithic times, but ran along the outside of one edge, away from the entrances, so the "arrows of *sha*" would not affect the inhabitants.
7. A basic knowledge of *feng shui* can thus cast light on some aspects of earth mysteries everywhere in the world. More generally, close attention to the landscape around an ancient site can very often clarify much about that site and its purpose and function. Notice the natural flow and character of the landscape, its heights and depths, and the way the human mind naturally follows the heights and valleys, and it becomes easier to step outside of the disenchanted mindset of the modern world and see the land as ancient peoples saw it.

Practical work

During the week you spend on this lesson, see what resources on *feng shui* you can find at libraries and on the internet. Decide how much you want to learn about the subject, and begin studying it if this seems appropriate to you. In the meantime, as you spend time outdoors, pay attention to the landscape in the terms just given. Are there hills that might channel the blue dragon current? Are there ripples and curves in the land that might channel the white tiger current? Do you notice "arrows of *sha*," and if so, what effect do they seem to have?

Question for reflection

What message might the shapes of the land where you live be communicating to you?

LESSON 15

The land as palimpsest

Seed thought

> Watkins saw straight through the surface of the landscape to a layer deposited in some remote prehistoric age. The barrier of time melted and, spread across the country, he saw a web of lines linking the holy places and sites of antiquity.
> —John Michell, *The View Over Atlantis*

Orientation

1. In ancient times, before the invention of paper, parchment made from sheepskin was a common writing material. Since it was expensive, scribes found that they could reuse it by scraping off the writing on an old piece of parchment and writing something else in its place. A piece of parchment scraped off and reused in this way was called a palimpsest. Scholars have found that they can very often read at least a little of the text that had been scraped off, because faint traces of the original writing remained behind.
2. In most parts of the world today, the land is like a palimpsest that has been scraped off repeatedly, leaving faint traces behind each time.

The buildings and roads visible today are the equivalent of the most recent writing on the palimpsest. Traces from earlier times can sometimes be spotted easily, though in other cases they can be much harder to find. The further back you go and the more frequent and ruthless the scraping, the more difficult it can be to see any trace of older layers, but sometimes very ancient traces have endured even in the most prosaic settings.

3. Human beings are not the only source of erasures. The forces of nature do this too, and sometimes the scraping in question is far more dramatic than anything our species can do. Any part of the world that was covered with ice sheets during an ice age, for example, was literally scraped clean by millions of tons of ice sliding slowly across the landscape. Sea level has risen and fallen, drowning wide regions and lifting others from under the sea. Volcanoes have blanketed whole regions with thick blankets of ash, climate change has turned forests into deserts and deserts into forests, and collisions between drifting continents have lifted sea bottoms and turned them into mountain peaks.

4. Every landscape, as a result, will display at least three layers of "writing." The first and most easily read layer consists of recent landscape features put there by modern means. Beneath that will be another layer, harder to read, which consists of traces left by people living on the land before the modern era. Beneath that, finally, will be the layer put there by natural forces before human beings came on the scene. Each of these three layers may be divided into many other layers—for example, the layer of earlier human presence may consist of a dozen or more layers left there by different eras and cultures, while the layer put there by natural forces may also be divided into different layers left there by one geological age following another.

5. When you begin investigating a landscape, the different layers of the palimpsest will appear all jumbled together, and it may take you hard work to sort out which feature belongs to which layer of time. Here, for example, is a conical hill covered with grass. Was it created as a dumping place for dirt and rock from an old mine a century ago? Was it put there by some more ancient people long before the ancestors of the present people arrived? Or is it a natural hill shaped by wind, water, and geological forces before human beings evolved? Some of the inner properties of the hill may vary considerably depending on the answer to this question.

6. Your inner senses will thus be of some help in sorting out the origins of the features in the landscape you are studying, but here in particular it needs to be remembered that your inner senses are no more infallible than your outer senses. Even if that conical mound feels to you like a Native American or Celtic mound, and you experience a Native American or Celtic presence there, it may turn out to be a natural hill or a heap of nineteenth-century mine tailings. That need not keep it from functioning as a sacred space for you, but knowing the difference between history and myth can keep you from making a fool of yourself in public.
7. With study and practice, you will find that it becomes possible to see or sense the way a landscape has changed over time. As you become skilled at this, you will find that your inner senses contribute to the process in subtler and more complex ways. The more you learn about the landscape, the more easily you will be able to do this, and in the process you will find it easier to make contact with the enchantment in the land.

Practical work

Visit your local public library and find at least one book on the geology of the region in which you live, at least one book on the prehistory of the same region, and at least one book that summarizes its known history. Read all three books. Afterwards, make it a habit of looking at the landscape around you and thinking about when any given feature on it might have come into being. Was it there before human beings, and if so, how far back before human beings? Was it there before the first people who left written records arrived in the region? If it is more recent than that, when in the history of the region might it have appeared?

Question for reflection

How many distinct layers of influence on the landscape can you perceive in the area you are studying?

LESSON 16

Mounds and earthworks

Seed thought

The way was steep and winding, with a hollow cup of the hills below it, and above it a bent so steep that Ralph could see but a few yards of it on his left hand; but when he came to the hill's brow and could look down on the said bent, he saw strange figures on the face thereof, done by cutting away the turf so that the chalk might show clear. A tree with leaves was done on that hill-side, and on either hand of it a beast like a bear ramping up against the tree; and these signs were very ancient.
—William Morris, *The Well at the World's End*

Orientation

1. Over much of the world, ancient peoples moved huge quantities of earth to build mounds and other earthen shapes for unknown purposes. Many of the world's most striking and mysterious sites consist of earthworks of one kind or another. Some of these, such as Ohio's Serpent Mount and England's Silbury Hill, are famous; others have a presence in local folklore but have rarely been heard of outside the

regions surrounding them; still others have been completely forgotten, and have to be tracked down by way of old books and records.
2. Because so many people nowadays have forgotten how to pay attention to the shape of the land, mounds and earthworks very often go unnoticed by the casual visitor. Some people who go to Stonehenge each year leave without ever noticing the ditch and bank that surrounds it or the two mounds within the ditch and bank to north and south of the famous standing stones. Where more obvious traces are lacking, it can take a perceptive eye to notice the signs that a mound, a ditch, or a bank might be the work of human beings rather than natural forces.
3. Earthworks vary from one part of the world to another and from one age to another. Archeologists have classified them into various categories. Knowing what types have been found in the area where you live can help you tell ancient earthworks from natural landforms or the effects of human activity in the industrial age. While there are many types of ancient earthworks, three in particular are worth discussing here: mounds, enclosures, and glyphs.
4. As the name suggests, mounds are masses of heaped and compacted earth, often built over a chamber of wood or stone and usually overgrown with grass, brush, or trees at the present day. They appear in many shapes and sizes, from low circular shapes a dozen feet across and a few feet high, concealing a tiny stone chamber and cremated remains, to long barrows well over 100 feet long and twenty feet high containing extensive stone-lined chambers. Some mounds were constructed as burial sites, but others show no signs of burials. Many were carefully constructed in multiple layers.
5. Enclosures are areas surrounded by banks and ditches. Here again, they are found in many shapes, sizes, and designs, and archeologists have worked out various categories for them. Some of them may have been fortifications meant to help defend against enemies, while the designs of other enclosures make no military sense and were apparently built for other reasons. Depending on the scale and age of an enclosure, it may be clearly visible, it may have vanished from sight over the centuries, or it may be anywhere between these extremes.
6. Glyphs are the most fragile of earthworks. These are images made by clearing away a surface layer of grass or soil to reveal an underlying layer of a different color. The chalk figures of England and the

strange lines of the Nazca plain in Peru are among the most famous glyphs that survive to the present. The Nazca plain is desert and the lines there have remained clear for many centuries despite neglect, but England's chalk figures have had to be cleared of grass by local people every few years since ancient times to keep them from being overgrown. Several once-famous chalk figures vanished in recent centuries once this duty was neglected.

7. Some areas of the world have hundreds of mounds and earthworks packed together in a small space. Others are relatively bare of earthen structures. Unless the area where you live has famous sites of this kind in it, you may need to do a great deal of digging in old historical or archeological records to find out if there were mounds or earthworks in your area, and where they were. Once you have located them, dowsing, psychometry, and other spiritual methods can be used to obtain more information about them.

Practical work

Go through your collection of information on local earth mysteries and see if there are any signs of mounds or earthworks in your area. If there are, research them during the week you spend on this lesson. Visit at least one of them if you have the chance. See how they fit into the broader landscape of the Unseen in the area where you live.

Whether or not there are mounds or earthworks in your area, read up on mounds and earthworks in other parts of the world, using local libraries or the internet as resources.

Question for reflection

How would you tell the difference between an artificial mound or earthwork and a natural feature, and what would the difference mean to you?

LESSON 17

Megaliths

Seed thought

In the exact center of the rabbit-nibbled turf an oblong boulder reclined upon its side. Hugh examined it. It was difficult to tell, so weather-worn it was, whether it was a natural outcrop or a tooled stone brought thither by the hand of man. The chalk, however, does not produce such stones as this, and Hugh, looking at the long narrow rock at his feet, guessed that it was one of those standing-stones of which Mona had spoken—a sighting-stone along a line of power.

—Dion Fortune, *The Goat-Foot God*

Orientation

1. The term "megalith" comes from the Greek language and simply means "big stone." The classic megaliths of northwestern Europe were exactly that, big stones that ancient people hauled long distances and set upright in the distant past. Nowadays the term "megalith" is used for nearly any ancient stone construction of unknown nature and purpose, no matter how large or small the stones

might be. Many of the mysterious stone chambers and alignments of New England are made of stones of modest size—very modest indeed compared to the mighty stones of Karnac or Stonehenge!—but the term "megalithic" is still commonly used for them.

2. Older books on megaliths often use distinctive names for certain kinds of megalithic constructions. A single upright standing stone is a menhir. A large stone propped up like a roof supported by three or four other stones is called a dolmen by some writers and a cromlech by others. (Under either name, they were once the stone chambers inside earthen mounds, but the earth was carried away by centuries of weathering.) A pair of stones with a single stone across the top, like the lintel of a door, is a trilithon. Stone chambers, walls, and alignments have no special names, although they are very common in some areas.

3. Different kinds of stones have different subtle reactions to the earth currents. The ancient peoples who built megalithic structures were accordingly precise in their choice of stones for a given site. In some cases, many of the stones in a site were sourced locally, but certain important stones such as the bluestones of Stonehenge were brought from considerable distances to play their roles in the structure. Large stones of a kind not found locally can thus be a telltale sign of a megalithic site.

4. It is sometimes difficult, however, to tell whether a large stone was put there by human beings or was left behind by natural forces. In areas that were covered by glaciers during the ice ages, stray lumps of rock called "erratics" by geologists were often carried many miles from their sources and left lying on the ground when the ice finally melted. If you live in an area that was covered by ice age glaciers, read up on local erratics before deciding that a stray stone must have been put there by some ancient culture. On the other hand, stone circles, stone chambers, or other structures are obviously not glacial relics!

5. An additional complication is that not all megaliths are still located where they were originally placed by their builders. It is far from uncommon for stones to be displaced or destroyed for the convenience of farmers or builders. There are technologies that can show patterns in the soil where a large stone was once located, but they are expensive and hard to access unless you happen to know a friendly archeologist. Fairly often researchers have had to use old writings

and drawings of a site to get some idea of what it was like before it was disrupted. Dowsing and psychometry can be used to supplement these resources.
6. Megalithic sites are very often associated with unusual experiences of many kinds. It is quite common, for example, for magnetic compasses to behave weirdly around standing stones, even when no trace of ordinary magnetism can be detected. Unexplained sounds and other odd effects have been detected with various kinds of scientific equipment, and people without benefit of complicated gear have found themselves affected by strange mental and physical conditions.
7. In dealing with megalithic sites, therefore, a certain amount of caution is wise. In at least some cases we appear to be dealing with the remnants of a forgotten technology based on principles that were lost centuries or millennia ago, with effects that are beyond our current ability to understand or predict. Local folklore about megalithic sites sometimes offers useful guidance, and should always be taken into account when deciding how to study a site where megalithic structures are present.

Practical work

Go through your collection of information on local earth mysteries and see if there are any megalithic structures in your area. If there are, research them during the week you spend on this lesson. Visit at least one of them if you have the chance. See how they fit into the broader landscape of the Unseen in the area where you live.

Whether or not there are megalithic structures in your area, read up on megalithic remains in other parts of the world, using local libraries or the internet as resources.

Question for reflection

What might the presence of a standing stone communicate to you?

LESSON 18

Shrines, temples, and churches

Seed thought

Places also exercise an important influence on occult operations; some spots upon the earth's surface are naturally highly magnetic. These have usually been discovered of old time by the ancients and their possibilities developed, and according to the type of development employed will be their influence at the present day. There is a very great difference between a place that has been used for initiations and one which has been used for evocatory rites involving blood sacrifice.
—Dion Fortune, *The Training and Work of the Initiate*

Orientation

1. From the most ancient times, human beings have set aside certain places as sacred and carried out rituals and other practices in those places. As nomadic customs gave way to more settled ways of living and the art of building came to be practiced, many of these places became the sites of special structures set aside for sacred purposes: shrines, temples, churches, and the like. In many cases these

structures came to be specially designed to receive and transmit the earth current, and became centers of power around which many legends gathered.
2. In many places, however, the connection between sacred structures and the subtle energies of the earth has been forgotten. As societies grew more complex, political and economic considerations very often took precedence over the old earth lore, and shrines, temples, and churches were built in places that lacked any connection to the earth magic. The sheer force of religious devotion can sometimes make up the difference, but if that falters, the result is an empty shell purporting to be a sacred structure.
3. In mapping out the geography of the Unseen in your area, therefore, it is crucial to recognize the difference between religious structures that have been placed on sacred ground, those on ordinary ground that have been charged by ongoing devotion, and those that have neither source of power and lack any connection to the subtle dimensions of the land.
4. The date of origin is a useful marker in many areas. In Western Europe, for example, the art of locating places for churches where the earth currents would flow freely remained in common use until the early sixteenth century. Many early Christian churches in these regions were deliberately placed on the site of Pagan temples or megalithic ruins to take advantage of the energies. Churches built before 1500 or so very often have some connection to the old earth magic, while those from afterwards—unless they were built on the site of an older church or temple—rarely do so. Thus very few American churches, for example, have any connection to the earth currents, since colonial settlement began only after the old earth lore was forgotten.
5. More recent religious structures with connections to the earth current were almost always built by newly founded religions or occult groups. The reason for this is quite simple: many new religions are founded by visionaries who are sensitive to the earth currents, and many occult traditions include methods that allow the earth currents to be sensed. This is among the reasons why new religions and occult teachings have displayed so much vitality in modern times, as compared to the religious mainstream: they have a source of energy the mainstream lacks.
6. To determine if a certain shrine, church, or temple in your area functions as a center of the earth current, dowsing and psychometry are

helpful, but there are other clues. Meditation and other forms of spiritual practice carried out in or immediately around the site will have a quality noticeably different from the same practices done elsewhere. A history of visionary experiences, miraculous healings, and other remarkable phenomena in and around the structure is another indication. With practice, you will find that it is tolerably easy to sense the difference between a sacred structure that has a connection to the earth currents and one that does not. Nothing feels quite so dead and empty as a church located purely for economic or practical reasons.
7. Even at the present time, some sacred buildings are properly located in places where the earth currents are strong, and efforts to rediscover the old earth lore of church and temple placement are ongoing. If this work goes well, there may come a time in the future when choosing a church or temple site without making sure of its connection to the earth currents will seem as absurd as building a house without connecting it to water, sewer, and power services. Until and unless that happens, researchers into earth mysteries will need to pay attention to the presence or absence of earth energies in the places of worship in the areas they study.

Practical work

During the week you spend on this lesson, look into the history of religious structures in your area and see whether there are any traces of traditional placement lore in any of the religious traditions that have been active there. Consider in this light the past and present places of worship in your area, and see if any of them show any sign of being connected to the earth currents and having a significant spiritual effect on their surroundings.

Whether or not there are old sacred sites in your area, read up on such places in other parts of the world, using local libraries or the internet as resources.

Question for reflection

What would make a place sacred or holy to you?

LESSON 19

Alignments 1—Leys

Seed thought

Imagine a fairy chain stretched from mountain peak to mountain peak, so far as the eye could reach, and paid out until it touched the high places of the earth at a number of ridges, banks, and knowls. Then visualise a mound, circular earthwork, or clump of trees, planted on these high points, and in low points in the valley, other mounds ringed round with water to be seen from a distance. Then great standing stones brought to mark the way at intervals, and on a bank leading up to a mountain ridge or down to a ford the track cut deep so as to form a guiding notch on the skyline as you come up.

—Alfred Watkins, *The Old Straight Track*

Orientation

1. One summer day in 1921, a man named Alfred Watkins was traveling across the Bredwardine Hills in rural Herefordshire, near the border between England and Wales. Watkins had grown up in the region and had an endless appetite for its folklore, traditions, and

antiquities—the knowledge that opens the doors to the enchantment of the land. That day, standing on a hilltop, he looked out over the countryside and realized that all the ancient sites he saw around him were placed on a handful of lines that ran dead straight across the landscape.

2. Watkins reported his discovery to a local society of naturalists that same year, and published a pamphlet, *Early British Trackways*, soon thereafter. In 1925 his most influential book on the subject, *The Old Straight Track*, saw print. His discoveries were rejected out of hand by the archeological establishment but attracted a wide circle of independent investigators who found it easy to replicate Watkins's experience in other parts of Britain, and in some other parts of the world as well. The arrangement of ancient sites in straight lines across the landscape has gone on to become a core subject of earth mysteries research.

3. Because so many of the places touched by the lines had the element "-ley" as part of their names, Watkins took to calling the alignments "leys." (In popular culture this has generally been modified into "ley lines.") Watkins's own interpretation of the leys was that they were an ancient system of land navigation, designed to make travel and trade possible in the days before maps and written itineraries. Standing stones, earthen mounds, notches cut into hills and ridges, pools placed so that they reflected the sky when seen from a ridgeline track, clusters of pines that reseeded themselves down through the centuries: all these were part of the system, guiding traders and pilgrims across the landscape of ancient Britain.

4. As Watkins and his fellow investigators pursued their quest to understand the ley system, however, it became clear that something stranger than land navigation was involved. Dowsers found that they could track leys across the landscape even if they didn't know a ley was present. Curious legends and strange experiences suggested that some influence or energy unknown to modern scientists followed the lines, and could be perceived by sensitive persons as they walked the lines.

5. Two important points need to be kept in mind whenever leys are considered. The first is that they are not part of the natural environment. They are artifacts, created by human beings in the distant past. As we have already learned, the natural lines of the earth current follow the curves of the landscape, not the straight alignments that Watkins discovered. In the palimpsest of the landscape, the leys are not the deepest layer. They may not even be the oldest human layer.

6. The second point, which unfolds from this, is that some places have leys and others do not. Watkins and his fellow investigators became skilled at telling the difference between actual leys and mere chance arrangements of points. There must be at least four ancient sites (many modern researchers require six) in an exact line within a relatively short distance, such as twenty miles. Evidence of an old trail, track, or road following the same line is helpful, but the crucial test involves walking the route of the suspected ley. Very consistently, an actual ley will have additional markers not found on the map, and the line will make sense as a route for foot travel.
7. As this suggests, ley walking is an essential part of this aspect of earth mysteries work. This is easy in countries such as England, where footpaths are common, and harder in other places where foot travel is less convenient. If you live in one of the latter regions, and the evidence suggests that leys exist in your area, it may take a great deal of walking even to find the places where a ley crosses the modern road system. Remember also that it is never wise to venture onto private property unless you have the permission of the landowner.

Practical work

As you compile your list of local earth mysteries, mark every site on a good map—an Ordnance Survey map in Britain, a USGS topographical map in the United States, and the equivalent in other countries. Alfred Watkins's advice is still sound; he recommended that each site be marked with a small circle in ink. See if four or more of the sites you locate form a straight line across the landscape. If so, consider walking as much of the alignment as you can. If other researchers have already gone looking for leys in your area, see what they found, and if a well-defined ley is among their discoveries, make time to walk it.

Whether or not there are alignments in your area, read up on those that have been found in other parts of the world, using local libraries or the internet as resources.

Question for reflection

Does Watkins's hypothesis that leys were ancient trackways seem plausible to you? Why or why not?

LESSON 20

Alignments 2—Spirit roads

Seed thought

"Now look at this map. You see Avebury?"

"Yes."

"That was the center of the old sun-worship. Now draw a line from Avebury to any other place where there are the remains of ancient worship, and anywhere along that line will be good for what you want."

—Dion Fortune, *The Goat-Foot God*

Orientation

1. One of the puzzles in earth mysteries research is the relation between the lines that Alfred Watkins discovered and another system of straight lines, also found in some parts of the world and absent in others. This second set of lines consists of dead straight roads extending out in various directions from sacred places, tombs, temples, and old churches. They have various names in the countries where they appear, but a good general term for them is "spirit roads."

2. Surviving examples of spirit roads are by and large much more recent than the tracks that Watkins researched. The examples in the Netherlands and Britain, for example, spread out from churches built in the Middle Ages, and the straight alignments that extend from Shinto shrines in Japan, marked by symbolic *torii* gates, seem to have been introduced around the tenth century. In the Andes, the system of forty straight *ceques* extending across the mountain landscape from the temple of the Sun in the Inca capital at Cuzco was not put in place until a few centuries before the Spanish conquest of 1542.
3. Other examples are older. In China, straight "spirit paths" that radiate from the tombs of emperors date to the beginning of the common era, while ancient Greek sacred roads extending from temples go back maybe 1000 years further. None seem to date back to Neolithic times, as Watkins's alignments do. This is another useful reminder that earth mysteries are not all of the same ancient date, and may embody the legacy of thousands of years of varying human interaction with the enchantments of the land.
4. Many but not all of these alignments from sacred sites have an uncanny association with the dead. In England, the Netherlands, and Germany, spirit roads were used to carry the bodies of the dead to church for funeral rites, and were often forbidden for any other use. They were typically given names that relate to death—the English examples, for example, were called "church roads" or "corpse roads," and the Dutch versions were *doodwegen*, "dead ways." The spirit paths extending from Chinese tombs were also obviously associated with the dead, and were considered unlucky for the living to use.
5. One consequence of this connection with the dead is that ghosts and other strange phenomena are often associated with these alignments. It is far from rare for local folklore to report that something ghostly is often seen moving along an old road, path, or track that goes to or from an old church or sacred site: for example, the phantom of a black dog may be seen running along some such route, or a glowing ball of light may appear moving through the air above the track. Such indications can help you identify an otherwise forgotten alignment.
6. If you live in an area that has ancient or medieval sacred sites in it, watch for alignments that radiate out from such a site for modest distances, rather than tracing long straight lines across the landscape as leys do. Spirit roads are more likely to involve actual roads, paths, or tracks than leys, and you may be able to identify them on that basis if

the local landscape has not been too heavily remodeled for the sake of automobile traffic.
7. Unlike leys or the curved lines that the earth current follows naturally, spirit roads are often considered in folklore to be unlucky or dangerous for the living to walk. One theory encountered in occult teachings, and also in ancient spiritual traditions such as Shinto, is that the influences that move along these paths are too intense for prolonged exposure. It can also be risky to perform spiritual work on such alignments. In the quote from Dion Fortune's *The Goat-Foot God* that begins this lesson, the speakers are seeking a location where certain powerful rituals can be performed. Before you try to imitate them, be sure you know what you are doing and have ample experience with similar practices in less potent settings.

Practical work

The process of marking down sites on a good map discussed in the previous lesson can also be helpful for revealing the presence of this second class of alignments, if you happen to live in a region where they exist. Look for old footpaths or narrow roads spreading out in many directions from a sacred place of some kind. Close attention to local folklore is also helpful, and if other researchers have already found a set of spirit roads in your area, their work can be very helpful as you assemble your collection of sites.

Whether or not there are spirit paths in your area, read up on examples in other parts of the world, using local libraries or the internet as resources.

Question for reflection

What thoughts and feelings come to mind when you reflect on the idea of straight line paths running across the landscape?

LESSON 21

Alignments 3—The earth and the heavens

Seed thought

The stone circles of Britain and the stone wheels of the North American Indians, the megalithic chambered mounds of Ireland and Europe, the temples of Mexico, Peru, Greece, Egypt, and the East; all these are found to have been orientated to the heavenly bodies. At certain moments of the year they were illuminated by sun, moon, or starlight, and in that form the heavenly gods entered their temples, contributing their powers to the magical rites performed there.
—John Michell and Christine Rhone, *Twelve-Tribe Nations and the Ancient Science of Enchanting the Landscape*

Orientation

1. The alignments we have discussed so far point toward sites on earth. Another class of important alignments, however, are oriented toward the heavens. Ancient peoples used the movements of the sun, the moon, and the planets against the background of the stars as compass, clock, and calendar. The skies were therefore of supreme

importance to them, and it comes as no surprise that many sites are aligned so that certain events in the heavens affect them at regular intervals over the course of the year.

2. The most common of these alignments were to the important stations of the sun. Over the course of the year, due to our planet's tilted axis, the points on the horizon where the sun appears to rise and set move north and south a considerable distance. Setting up a stone circle so that the sun rises over a specific stone at midsummer, or orienting a mound so that the sun shines all the way down its central passage to the end when it rises on the day of midwinter, allowed ancient peoples who lacked a written calendar to keep precise track of the seasons. Other sites lined up on sunrise or sunset at other times of the year.

3. The sun, however, is not the only thing alignments track. Positions of the moon, especially those that allowed ancient peoples to track the cycle that led to eclipses, are often found in ancient sites. The rising and setting of certain clearly visible groups of stars, such as the Pleiades, at specific seasons of the year guide another set of alignments. The ancients paid close attention to the heavens, and almost any regularly repeating celestial event might play a role in an alignment in an ancient site.

4. Particular alignments to the heavens tend to be found in specific regions. Students of Native American archeoastronomy have noted, for example, that in the northeastern states, sites aligned on midsummer sunrise are found in a region that extends from the eastern end of Long Island through Connecticut and the lower Hudson valley of New York to the Catskill Mountains. Further north in Putnam County, New York, sites tend to be aligned on midwinter sunrise instead. In other areas, sites may be aligned on many different heavenly bodies.

5. Once such a tradition is established, it can remain in place for a very long time. The long barrows of Neolithic Britain and Ireland are aligned at various points on the eastern horizon, for instance, and archeologists have suggested that they were positioned so that the sun would shine all the way down the barrow's interior tunnel to its end at a particular date. The same custom was still in use thousands of years later in early British and Irish Christian churches, many of which are aligned so that the sun shines down the nave of the church on the day assigned to the saint in whose honor the church was named.

6. Computer programs and other resources can be used to find the specific directions at which the sun, the moon, and important stars rise and set at different times of the year at your latitude, and books and websites on archeoastronomy—the scholarly discipline that studies ancient ways of making sense of the heavens—can give you information on these. It can be a real education to apply these resources to sites in your area and see what you find.
7. The great challenge in using such resources is that the earth's surface is so rarely flat. A hill or valley east or west of a site can change the position of sunrise or sunset by several degrees, and very often there is no easy way to work this out except by going to the site at the date in question and watching the heavens. On the other hand, this is well worth doing for its own reasons. To stand at an ancient site waiting for the sun to rise or set is to enter into the same activity as the people who built and used the site in the past, and can lead to important insights.

Practical work

During the week you spend on this lesson, look over the list of earth mysteries sites in your area that you have identified, and see whether any of them might be aligned on the heavens. Sometimes this is obvious—a menhir outside a stone circle in the direction of midsummer sunrise, or the door of a stone chamber pointing straight to the place where the Pleiades rise at a particular season, are hard to miss—while sometimes it can be much subtler.

In the meantime, using local libraries or the internet, find resources on archeoastronomy, and see if you can locate anything dealing with sites in your area. If you can identify a seasonal alignment to a site in your area and go there at the right time to watch the heavens, do so.

Question for reflection

How does the land in the region you are studying seem to relate to the rising and setting of the sun, moon, planets, and stars?

LESSON 22

Relics out of place

Seed thought

Almost from the time of the first American settlers, people have been discovering old coins in unlikely places. Roman coins, especially, have turned up in farmers' fields, on beaches, and elsewhere across the country. It seems that the Romans and other pre-Columbian peoples either strayed far beyond the Gates of Hercules or a lot of numismatists had holes in their pockets.
—William R. Corliss, *Ancient Man: A Handbook of Puzzling Artifacts*

Orientation

1. Every culture has a set of beliefs about its own past. The cultures of the modern industrial world are no exception. Every culture's beliefs about the past provide the filter through which people in that culture interpret the present, and here, too, modern industrial cultures are no different. Put another way, every culture's account of its past tells a story, and that story defines the nature of history and human existence for those people who believe that the story is true. If the story

turns out not to match the facts, very often, the facts are ignored—and this, too, is true in the modern industrial world.

2. In industrial societies, the most common belief about the past insists that for countless generations, human beings lived in ignorance and squalor, never asking even the most obvious questions about the physical world around them, but believing foolish fables instead. Then, some 5000 years ago, they suddenly invented agriculture, architecture, metallurgy, and writing, and then stopped. About 400 years ago, the people in one small corner of the world, Western Europe, launched the age of exploration, invented modern science, and began the trajectory of progress that someday soon will take us or our descendants to the stars.

3. There are several major problems with this rather odd belief system. Among the most important is that artifacts keep turning up to contradict it. Some of these artifacts suggest that ancient people crossed oceans and brought continents into contact long before today's conventional wisdom would allow. Some of them suggest that a range of unexpected technologies were known far earlier than current beliefs accept. Some of them, finally, point to the existence of complex urban societies that thrived during the ages when the accepted version of the past insists that every human being lived in tribal savagery.

4. Out-of-place artifacts of these kinds have become part of earth mysteries research for two reasons, one purely practical, the other of deeper importance. The purely practical reason is that the two fields overlap substantially in their subject matter, the skills needed to explore them, and their intrinsic interest. Sites and stories are of equal importance to both, the same hard work of library and internet research and close observation of surviving traces is required by both, and the passion that drives investigators to explore alternative history and prehistory differs only in detail from the comparable passion that motivates the student of earth mysteries.

5. The deeper reason for the connection between out-of-place artifacts and earth mysteries is that most ancient peoples, unlike modern industrial societies, understood the world in ways that make room for the subtle factors that earth mysteries researchers study. Close attention to the Unseen was common practice in ancient civilizations, and even in the era when European explorers and colonists founded their first settlements in the New World, knowledge of the hidden side of existence had not entirely been suppressed. Some of

the sites central to alternative visions of history and prehistory are places where the Unseen manifests, and so are of interest to students of earth mysteries more generally.
6. The standard tools of earth mysteries research are valuable assets in this branch of study, but even more caution is necessary here than elsewhere in using visionary experience as a guide. Many alternative visions of the past have attracted strong passions, and these leave their mark in the Unseen; so do popular entertainments that offer vivid visual imagery. It is quite possible to seek imagery from ancient Atlantis and end up with something from a Hollywood production on the subject, engraved on the inner planes by the rapt attention of audiences.
7. You may find it helpful in this branch of earth mysteries research to read about other explorations into alternative history and prehistory, and watch the way that the same evidence can be used to bolster any number of competing theories. Keep this in mind as you try to tease out the origins of some enigmatic site and you will be less likely to mistake the struggle to prove some particular claim for the deeper and more meaningful quest to come closer to the meaning of a mystery.

Practical work

During the week you spend on this lesson, look over the list of earth mysteries sites in your area that you have identified, and see whether any of them might have connections to long-distance contacts, advanced technologies, or lost civilizations not currently accepted by academic historians. In the meantime, using local libraries or the internet, research any of these subjects that interest you, and see whether any of them are linked in any way to the area you are studying.

Whether or not you can find anything of this kind in your area, read up on examples in other parts of the world, using local libraries or the internet as resources.

Question for reflection

What aspects of the history you were taught in school never made sense to you?

LESSON 23

Landscape patterns

Seed thought

The Glastonbury Zodiac is thus a powerful and haunting symbol, evoking ancient memories. Since [Katherine] Maltwood's time its effigies have been tended and preserved by her local followers, and the concept of a landscape zodiac is now established in many minds. Whether or not she was right in her interpretation of it, her perception of an astrological pattern at Glastonbury is well founded and effective.
—John Michell and Christine Rhone, *Twelve-Tribe Nations and the Ancient Science of Enchanting the Landscape*

Orientation

1. Some researchers into earth mysteries have claimed to see patterns traced out over entire landscapes by the labor of ancient peoples. One of the first scholars to study the archaic sites of Britain, pioneering archeologist Rev. William Stukeley, argued that the landscape around the stone circles of Avebury had been marked with avenues of standing stones and subsidiary stone circles, forming the image of

a serpent and a circle more than three miles across. While many of the stones visible in Stukeley's time were destroyed by farmers afterwards, enough remain to suggest that he may have been right.

2. Far more controversial are the claims of Katharine Maltwood. An artist and sculptor active in England between the two world wars, she believed that she had discovered the key to the Arthurian legends in a vast map of the zodiac traced out in the landscape near the town of Glastonbury. In her vision, streams, ancient trackways and roads, the boundaries of fields left unchanged from the Middle Ages, and other enduring markings on the land set out the twelve signs of the zodiac in a circle eight miles across.

3. Some earth mysteries researchers still accept the reality of Maltwood's landscape zodiac, and other zodiacs have been identified in a few other places, especially in Britain. Most students of earth mysteries, however, point out that the logic used to trace landscape zodiacs is not that different from the kind of imaginative pattern recognition that leads people to look at an inkblot and see two bats having a romantic interlude. A middle ground is occupied by those who see Maltwood's theory and its equivalents as an attempt to interpret the presence of the Unseen in the everyday world: symbolically and poetically true, but not literally so.

4. The more speculative end of ley research has generated its share of apparent large-scale landscape patterns. Some earth mysteries researchers have traced alignments for hundreds of miles, noticing that (for example) churches placed along a given line are commonly assigned to the same saint, or have other symbolic resonances. Others have tried to map out ley patterns over continents or the entire world. Each of these schemes has its supporters; each also has critics who argue that the evidence cannot be stretched that far.

5. The same difference of opinion applies to attempts to see large-scale patterns in the landscape unrelated to leys. There are many of these in the contemporary earth mysteries field, ranging in scale from a few miles across to grand patterns of spherical geometry embracing the entire planet. Each such theory has its small circle of proponents confronting a much larger circle of the unconvinced. In most cases it is impossible to disprove a claim of this kind—how can you be sure that any given set of patterns on the land *wasn't* put there in ancient times?—but proof is just as elusive in practice.

6. As a rule of thumb, the smaller an apparent landscape pattern is, the more likely it is to have been intended by the people who built the structures that form it. Stukeley's serpent and circle was well within the capacity of the ancient people of Britain to conceive and create using the stone, bone, and wooden tools found in excavations at Avebury. Some other proposed structures are on a scale so gigantic that it would be a challenge to build such a structure even with the latest modern technology.
7. The claim has of course been made many times that ancient people may have had technology equal or superior to that of modern industrial society. Some enigmatic traces seem to support this suggestion. Yet it is important to avoid the circular reasoning that takes an apparent landscape pattern as proof that the advanced technology needed to plan and construct it must have existed, and then takes the supposed existence of the advanced technology as proof that the apparent landscape pattern must have been deliberately planned and constructed. It is always possible that you are staring at inkblots instead.

Practical work

During the week you spend on this lesson, use the internet or your local library to see if your area has been identified as the site of a local landscape pattern, or as part of a larger pattern. If so, consider the evidence for and against it. If not, look into at least one other large-scale landscape pattern somewhere else in the world, and come to your own conclusions as to how seriously to take the theory its proponents advance. In the meantime, assess the sites in your area to see if any large-scale pattern is evident in their arrangement.

Question for reflection

What evidence for a large-scale landscape pattern would seem conclusive to you?

LESSON 24

The language of the land

Seed thought

In all the world there is nothing quite like the gaunt ruin which Henry James said "stands as lonely in history as it does on the great plain." Immense and still, it seems beyond man, beyond mortality. In its presence, within those silent circles, one feels the great past all around. One can almost see and hear ... until one tries to imagine precisely *what* sights and sounds animated that place, what manner of men moved there, in that inconceivably remote past when it was new.

—Gerald Hawkins, *Stonehenge Decoded*

Orientation

1. In trying to read the patterns left on the landscape by ancient peoples, earth mysteries researchers face much the same challenge as linguists who hope to decipher an unknown ancient script. The forms survive but the meanings do not, and a great deal of work has to go into collecting all the available data and attempting to relate the scattered

fragments to themselves, and to other sources of information, before the first guesses at the original meaning of the text become possible.

2. The history of the decipherment of ancient scripts is littered with failed attempts made too soon, on the basis of too few data points, or under the influence of some popular belief that turns out to be hopelessly wrong. The same thing is true in the field of earth mysteries. Read through books written about famous ancient sites and you can find plenty of grand conclusions based on too little evidence, too many assumptions, and too much attention to whatever set of notions about the past was most popular when any given book was written.

3. Fitting the remnants of the distant past into an arbitrary scheme of this kind is easy. Listening to what those remnants themselves are able to communicate is much harder. If that message from the past happens to talk about things that cannot be understood from within the worldview of today's materialist sciences, as usually happens, the difficulty becomes even greater. That gives students of earth mysteries who are not fettered to a materialist viewpoint an advantage, but it's all too easy to lose that advantage and plunge into some other belief system that gets in the way of listening to the land.

4. The skill that will do the most to keep you from falling into this trap is that of keeping an open mind. This doesn't mean believing everything you hear or read, as some people seem to think. What it requires is the ability to postpone judgment—to look at competing claims, and gather evidence relating to those claims, without accepting or rejecting any of them.

5. Suppose, for example, that you are investigating the Newport Tower in Rhode Island.* The archeological mainstream insists that it was built in colonial times as a windmill, though the evidence for this is slight and betrays circular reasoning. A number of researchers have proposed several alternative theories for its construction, some more plausible than others. The evidence surrounding the tower is fragmentary, contradictory, and inconclusive—as is usually the case in earth mysteries research.

6. If you accept any one of the theories and set yourself to find evidence to confirm it, you can doubtless build a case for that theory, but it will

---

*See Additional Lesson 3, pp. 215–221, for more on this enigmatic site.

only convince people who already agree with you. This is what too many students of earth mysteries do, and it has played a crucial role in keeping the field as confused as it is. If you keep an open mind and gather evidence without having any of the theories in mind, on the other hand, you are more likely to spot a detail that contradicts one theory or gives crucial support to another.
7. Put simply, it is necessary to listen to the language of the land, so that you hear what it has to say, instead of deciding what you want it to say and putting words into its mouth. You must learn to treat the land as a partner in a dialogue, not a blank screen on which to project your own ideas and meanings. Listening to what sites have to teach is a slow process and requires much patience, but it has an advantage that other approaches lack: it can teach you things you don't already know, and perhaps have never dreamed of knowing.

Practical work

During the week you spend on this lesson, look over the evidence you have gathered for the sites that interest you in the area you are studying. Study the data, and see what patterns stand out. Can you create a theory to explain the nature and distribution of the sites? When were they made, who made them, and why? Once you have done this, see if you can disprove your theory. Put yourself in the place of a critic who has no reason to agree with you, and look for all the weak places in your theory. Look especially for places where a little more investigation might bring up evidence that either supports or challenges your ideas. Consider doing that further investigation, and see what you find.

Question for reflection

If the landscape around you is speaking, what is it trying to say to you?

UNIT THREE

STORIES

LESSON 25

Overview of stories

Seed thought

> The wellspring of knowledge flowed from her lips on those evenings. She preserved the tribe's treasure under her white hair. Behind her gently furrowed old brow dwelt the memory and mind of the village. Anyone who knew any spells and stories had learned them from her.
> —Hermann Hesse, *The Glass Bead Game*

Orientation

1. Stories are the threads that tie together the present and the past. They are the raw material from which each of us builds an image of the world. By listening to the stories that have been told over the years in any part of the world, we can catch echoes of how people in the past understood the land around them. By paying attention to the stories that are still being told today, and comparing them with the ones that have dropped out of popular memory and are preserved only in old books, we can understand something of the way that a community's

relationship to the land has changed over time. All of this is relevant to the work of the student of earth mysteries.

2. Modern industrial cultures divide their stories into a set of categories, and assign these categories different levels of respectability. Among those categories are history, legend, and myth. Most people in our disenchanted time think that history is true, legends are partly true and partly false, and myth is false. They are mistaken, but it is important to recognize the meaning hidden behind the common assumptions of our time. What divides history from legend and legend from myth is the relation of different kinds of stories to enchantment.

3. History is our name for stories that are completely disenchanted and exist in a world of dead matter. Legend is our name for stories that are partly disenchanted, and myths are those stories that are wholly enchanted, and exist in a world full of life, consciousness, and meaning. Thus a story counts as history only if it describes events caused by human beings acting on each other or a world of dead matter, or by the world acting in a lifeless and purposeless way. Should it fail to fit within these narrow limits, it is called a legend if it is mostly about human beings, and a myth if it is mostly about spiritual beings.

4. Myths and legends have obvious importance to the student of earth mysteries, but history is also important. All stories, including those that have been forced within the narrow limits of the disenchanted consciousness, have something to offer in your quest. The history of Ireland has as much to teach about the subtle dimensions of the Irish land as do the legends of the Fianna or the mythic events of the *Book of Invasions*, just as the history of New England echoes the legends of the colonial era and the mythic narratives of the native peoples. As you explore the stories of the land where you live, keep watch for the same principle at work.

5. Some stories are detached from the land. These are the tales that turn up nearly everywhere on earth. They are valuable in other ways, but they have less to teach the earth mysteries researcher than other stories. The ones that have the most to communicate to the present subject are those that are tied to specific locations. It is one thing to find out that a piece of history, legend, or myth is remembered in the region where you are working. It is quite another to discover that the events of the story are related to some specific place in that region.

6. "Where did it happen?" is a question always worth keeping in mind when you are researching stories. You may be surprised to

find that whether something actually happened in a given place is less important than whether people believed that it happened there. Nonetheless this is quite true, and reflects a truth about stories. Human beings are storytelling creatures, and one of the ways we use stories is to pass on truths about the land. Whether or not a certain event actually happened in a certain place, the connection between event and place tells you that it is the kind of place where people in the past sensed that something of that kind could happen.

7. Surviving tribal peoples around the world still use myths and legends this way deliberately, as a means to pass on the secrets of the land to each new generation. In the world's industrial countries, this same custom has not quite disappeared, though few people realize that this is what is happening when parents or grandparents tell their children stories about a place, or people in a pub pass on stories and urban legends about the town where they live. Pay attention to the presence of stories in a place and you can often catch important clues about the enchantments of the land where you live.

Practical work

During the week you spend on this lesson, begin to collect stories about the area you are investigating if you have not already done so. Include the history of the area as well as the legends and myths associated with it, and do not neglect rumors and whatever stories you heard growing up, however odd or pointless they may seem. Wherever possible, identify specific locations associated with the stories; if a historical battle was fought at this river crossing or a local legend refers to that mountain, make sure to include these details in your record.

Question for reflection

What are the stories that matter most to you?

LESSON 26

The historical landscape

Seed thought

The historical event in itself, however important, does not remain in the popular memory, nor does its recollection kindle the poetic imagination save insofar as the particular historical event closely approaches a mythical model.
— Mircea Eliade, *Cosmos and History*

Orientation

1. It may seem odd at first glance to think of the history of a region or a country as part of a landscape of stories. Many of us were taught in school to think of history as "what actually happened" and to draw a hard line between history and the other kinds of stories that help trace the human experience of the land. It takes close attention to the work that historians actually do to see just how close their art is to any other kind of storytelling.
2. To begin with, history is never just "what actually happened." Everything that actually happened in any small town on an average week, if it was all recorded in detail, would fill many volumes.

The work of the historian is to pick and choose among the many events that happened in some specific place and time, selecting those that communicate something important about that place and time. What makes those events important? The story that the historian is trying to tell, using those events as incidents in a narrative.

3. A historian who wants to write about how the American colonies freed themselves from British rule will thus choose one set of events to discuss; a historian who wants to show how social habits changed over time in the American colonies during those same years may choose a completely different set of events. A novelist who is writing a mystery story, similarly, will choose one set of incidents to present in the story, while another novelist writing a romance may choose a different set of incidents. The sole difference between the historian and the novelist is that all the events the historian uses must have actually happened.

4. Yet historians do not write or research in a vacuum. Their views on what happened in the past are shaped by the work of other historians, and also by the hopes, fears, and ideas of people in the present time. That makes the historical writing of each generation a mirror of that generation's thoughts and feelings. Read half a dozen histories of the same subject written in as many different decades, and you can watch the way the authors respond to the pressures of their own time as well as the evidence from the past. The less evidence from the past there is, in turn, the more present-day concerns will shape the historical vision of each era.

5. As you listen to the stories of the region you are studying, then, reading several histories of that region is a good place to start. Choose one or two recent histories, and then find and read older histories as well, going back as far as you can. If you live in a place that has written histories dating from many centuries ago, make sure to include one of those—the different perspective on the past is worth having. Get a sense of what people in different eras have considered important about the past.

6. As you do this, it is important to include what mainstream historians like to call "pseudohistory"—that is to say, alternative histories that do not agree with current ideas about the past. Alternative views, even if they appear to be contradicted by the facts, are still part of the landscape of stories that people have told about the part of the world you are studying. The same open mind you cultivated while

considering competing claims about ancient sites is worth putting to work here as well. Accept alternative histories as part of the landscape of stories that reflects the human experience of the region you are studying, and see what they have to teach.

7. It is equally important not to assume in advance that the historical narrative presented by mainstream scholarship is true—or, for that matter, false. Treat it as a story, one that is of great cultural importance to the society that tells it. In our times, history fills many of the same roles that myth and legend once filled: it is the collection of stories that claims to explain where we came from, how we got here, and where we are headed. Those stories may use documented facts as their raw material, but they remain stories—and it is always possible that a different story, assembling an alternative set of incidents to make a different point, may have at least as much insight and wisdom to offer.

Practical work

During the week you spend on this lesson, if you have not already done so, obtain several histories of the area you are investigating. Choose at least one that is old enough to be considered outdated by today's historians, and if you can, at least one that presents an alternative view far enough from the mainstream to be considered "pseudohistory." Begin reading them, with an eye toward what they have to say about the region.

Question for reflection

What historical events make a difference to you personally?

LESSON 27

The mythic landscape

Seed thought

Mankind may have grown out of myths simply as explanations of the universe; but its need for myth as dramatization of nature's processes, as shapes to feed the imagination, as foci for seasonal awareness, is probably as great as ever.
—Ross Nichols, *An Examination of Creative Myth*

Orientation

1. The myths of any land are keys to the subtle energies and states of consciousness native to that land. This is true even when, as often happens, the myths in question were brought by settlers from elsewhere. Stories, like families, absorb the culture and ambience of a new environment over time. Know the myths that have taken root in a region or a country, and you have access to crucial insights into the inner dimensions of the land. To do this, however, it is necessary to get past certain barriers that modern ideologies have put in place.
2. One of the most important of these barriers is the lazy modern habit of thinking that the word "myth" means a story that is not true.

The Greek word *muthos*, from which our word "myth" descends, simply meant "story." In later times it came to mean the important stories, the ones that passed on important truths about the gods and the nature of the world. Later still, after the spread of Christianity, it was redefined again to refer only to the stories that had been important to the old Pagan religions, not to the stories that had the same role in the new faith—and more recently still, with the spread of dogmatic materialism, it came to be used for all stories about gods and the nature of the world that contradicted modern materialist beliefs.

3. By contrast, occultists recognize that all myths contain truths. Those occultists who also belong to a religious faith are especially attentive to the sacred stories of their own tradition, but they recognize that the sacred stories of other traditions also have truths to communicate. Those truths may or may not be literal—when Psalm 24 says "Lift up your heads, O ye gates," King David wasn't claiming that the city gates of Jerusalem literally had movable heads that would raise their chins on request!—and so an important part of dealing with sacred stories from any tradition involves figuring out when to take them literally and when to recognize the presence of metaphors and symbolism.

4. Another important barrier to understanding myths is the mistaken idea that all myths are about some single subject, and can be interpreted by translating them into that subject's terms. All through the nineteenth and early twentieth centuries, for example, many scholars argued that all myths were about astronomy. They were quite correct, of course, that the cycles of the heavens are often encoded in myths, but they were quite mistaken when they insisted that these were the only things that myths can teach.

5. Myths are the stories that matter, and they can matter in many different ways. Most myths, in fact, contain multiple layers of meaning. Only a few centuries ago, Jewish and Christian scholars agreed that every verse in the Bible contains at least four different meanings—a literal meaning, a moral meaning, a philosophical meaning, and a mystical meaning—and all of these were considered worth studying. In exactly the same way, it is quite common for ancient Greek myths to have historical, astronomical, agricultural, magical, and spiritual meanings all at once, and ancient Greek scholars such as Porphyry left commentaries on certain passages in Homer showing how these can be unpacked from the narrative.

6. This follows from the nature of myths. Storytelling is the oldest human information storage technology. Countless ages before the invention of writing, people learned to use stories to pass on the knowledge that mattered to each new generation. Remembering rhymed and rhythmic stories is hardwired into human genetics at this point, which is why you can probably still remember the nursery rhymes you grew up with, and likely have to make an effort not to repeat them in the same singsong tones you heard in early childhood! Many millennia of experimentation and practice made mythic narratives into an extremely subtle and flexible way of encoding information into vivid stories, and it requires equal subtlety to understand them.
7. As you begin to explore the myths that have put down roots into the area you are exploring, then, it is important not to assume in advance that you know what they have to teach. This is especially true of sacred stories you grew up with, whether you believe in them or not. Take the time to read them from original sources—many myths are far more complex and many-faceted than the watered-down versions common in today's culture. Think about what they could mean, but avoid forcing a meaning on them.

Practical work

During the week you spend on this lesson, focus your attention on whatever mythologies have been believed in the area you are studying. Include the sacred stories of present-day religions as well as those of older religions. Compare them with what you have already learned about the history of the area, and see what connections you can draw.

Question for reflection

What narratives are important enough to you that they could be called your myths?

LESSON 28

Myths and archetypes

Seed thought

There are no conclusive arguments against the hypothesis that these archetypal figures are endowed with personality at the outset and are not just secondary personifications. In so far as the archetypes do not represent mere functional relationships, they manifest themselves as *daimones*, as personal agencies. In this form they are felt as actual experiences and are not "figments of the imagination," as rationalism would have us believe.
—C. G. Jung, *Symbols of Transformation*

Orientation

1. The word "archetype" was brought back into common use in modern languages by the famous psychologist Carl Jung. In his work with psychiatric patients, Jung found that many of their troubles could not be traced back to ordinary personal experiences. Instead, the patients were having to cope with vivid, powerful images and presences that appeared to them as though from outside their minds. These images

and presences, Jung found, could also be traced in ancient myths and legends and in spiritual and occult traditions.

2. Jung came to believe that behind the ordinary, personal unconscious mind each of us has—the storehouse of forgotten memories and repressed experiences—there lay a much vaster collective unconscious mind that is shared by all human beings. Where the contents of the personal unconscious were once conscious, and have fallen into the unconscious because they were too painful or unpleasant to keep in consciousness, the contents of the collective unconscious have never been conscious. We can become aware of their reflections in our minds or in the creations of other minds—in stories, for example, or works of art—but we can never experience them directly.

3. The archetypes are the most important contents of the collective unconscious. They are older than our species. They are basic patterns of experience that reach far back into the prehistoric past, and link to the instincts we share with other animals, and they provide the basic vocabulary of concepts with which every human being approaches the world. They come into play in most of the basic relationships of human life. An infant clinging to the mother, a teenager falling helplessly in love, a soldier finding the courage to face the enemy, a parent raising a child, an elder facing the end of life—all of these are being guided and directed by archetypes.

4. The factor that makes archetypes especially important in the work of earth mysteries research is that since they are basic concepts that come naturally to the human mind, they appear over and over again in stories of every variety. Know that the Wise Old Man is an archetype, for example, and you will begin to recognize its presence everywhere, in novels, movies, myths, and legends, as well as dreams and visionary experiences, and in your own reactions to people who more or less fit the archetypal image.

5. There is no simple, straightforward list of the archetypes, nor will there ever be one: the deep places of the human mind are more elusive than that. Nor are archetypes always the same from place to place. Pay attention to the myths that have been believed in the area you are studying and you will quickly get a sense of what archetypes are active there. It also helps to learn something about myths generally, because it very often happens that archetypes that show up in the myths of one culture are found in less exalted settings in other cultures.

6. An example may be helpful here. Consider Paul Bunyan, the giant lumberman of American legend, and his equally titanic ox. The jocular folktales that surround Bunyan and Babe the blue ox may seem worlds away from myth, but the primal giant and his bull, cow, or ox is a pairing found in stories worldwide. Norse myth, for instance, begins with the frost giant Ymir and the cow Audhumla, who come into being out of the mists of Ginnungagap at the dawn of time. Nor is it irrelevant that William Blackstone, the first European settler in what is now Rhode Island and an unquestionably historical figure, appears in local legend riding a bull.*

7. The archetype that pairs the first man with a cow, bull, or ox can be traced back many centuries and found over much of the world, but it takes varied forms in different parts of the world. Gaining a sense of this and other archetypes it is easier to recognize the presence of mythic imagery in legend, history, and folk tradition. This in turn is an important skill to cultivate in learning to read the landscape of stories that shapes human consciousness in the area you are studying, and provides the context from which sites and phenomena draw much of their meaning.

Practical work

During the week you spend on this lesson, read at least one book of myths from a part of the world far from the area you are studying. Consider also reading an introductory book about archetypes, such as Jung's *Man and His Symbols*. If you are already familiar with Jung's ideas, consider reading a more serious book on archetypes or Jungian psychology.

Question for reflection

What archetypes might be active in your life and surroundings at present?

---

*See Sample Exploration 1, pp. 203–207, for more about this intriguing figure.

LESSON 29

The legendary landscape 1—Legends of the past

Seed thought

The same type of story [as the Arthurian legends] can be traced through many a mythology and scholars collate them, tracing the common factors in widely diversified schools and traditions. This is valuable because knowledge is never without value. There is the question of collating legends first with one another, and secondly, with other traditions.
—Dion Fortune, *The Arthurian Formula*

Orientation

1. Between history and myth, like a borderland between two kingdoms, lies the territory of legend. Legends differ from histories in that most of the events they describe did not actually happen, and those that did happen have become filled with an archetypal energy they did not necessarily have at the time. Legends differ from myths in that they recount stories of human beings rather than gods or legendary creatures, and the action is set in places that can be found

on ordinary maps. Think of them as archetypal stories using the ordinary world as raw material.
2. Legends fall more or less into two categories, which we can describe roughly as legends of the past and legends of the present. The boundary between the two categories is far from exact, since past and present intertwine in our experience. As a working rule, however, a story is set in the past if you can use phrases like "back then, things were different" when talking about it, without humor or irony. A story is set in the present if you can imagine it taking place right now, within a few miles of the place where you are reading this, without the least sense of absurdity or incongruity.
3. Legends of the past sometimes assign mythic roles to historical figures, and sometimes assign equally archetypal qualities to figures who never lived and, in some cases, never could have lived. In the United States, for example, the gigantic lumberman Paul Bunyan who features in so many tall tales of the north woods was never an actual person, while Johnny Appleseed, who has as large a role in frontier legend, was entirely historical—his name was John Chapman, his birth and death are matters of public record, and he actually did many of the things attributed to him in the stories. In the same way, King Richard the Lionhearted and Robin Hood are both major figures in English medieval legend; the first was entirely historical and did many of the things for which he is credited, while no trace of the latter has ever been found outside the realms of story.
4. What makes a legend, in other words, is not the historical reality or lack of it or the characters and events it describes. What makes a legend is the conjunction between a story about the past and the archetypal patterns discussed in the previous lesson. A legend is a story that should be true, according to the deep structures of consciousness, whether or not it is true in any historical sense. The United States should have had a Paul Bunyan and a Johnny Appleseed, just as England should have had a Richard Coeur de Lion and a Robin Hood. Whether or not these individuals happened to live in historical time is irrelevant to the collective unconscious of their respective countries.
5. The same is true of every other part of the world. Learn the legends of a country, and you can glimpse clues to the deep structures of consciousness that shape the thinking of the human and nonhuman inhabitants of that country. The same is true on a smaller scale,

for legends very often focus on areas much smaller than a nation. American states, British counties, and the provinces and departments of other countries very often have legends of their own; so do individual towns, rural places, and neighborhoods in cities. The collective unconscious is not a vague mass in which everything is mixed together all anyhow. It is at least as richly structured and textured as the material world—maybe more so.

6. Just as mythic figures very often appear in contexts that seem very far removed from mythology in the strict sense of the word, not all legends are obviously legendary. The border between legend and history is just as difficult to trace as the corresponding border between legend and myth. The biographies of most famous people have been edited to at least some extent to fit with the archetypes other people have projected on them. It can be educational to read biographies of the same person by two or more writers who assign different archetypes to their subject, and see how this editing process works!

7. Which historical figures have been selected out of the past to play a role in popular beliefs about history tells at least as much of their legendary roles as do any of the details of those figures' lives. In any period of history, in any place in the world, there are heroes and rascals, lovers and warriors, saints, sinners, and eccentrics. Notice which of these are seen as important in the present day, and you know which legendary patterns are more emphasized than others in the narratives of the area.

Practical work

During the week you spend on this lesson, focus your attention on the legendary past of the area you are studying. Try to get a clear sense of what people today believe about the past of the area, and what people in earlier times believed about their own past. Be sure to include historical figures as well as more obviously legendary characters. See what conclusions you can begin to draw about the nature of the area you have chosen to study.

Question for reflection

What messages do the legends of the area you are studying have for you today?

LESSON 30

The legendary landscape 2—Legends of the present

Seed thought

> In common with age-old folk legends about lost mines, buried treasure, omens, ghosts, and Robin Hood-like outlaw heroes, urban legends are told seriously, circulate largely by word of mouth, are generally anonymous, and vary considerably in particular details from one telling to another, while always preserving a central core of traditional elements or "motifs."
> —Jan Harold Brunvand, *The Vanishing Hitchhiker*

Orientation

1. Not all legends have to do with the past. The stories that circulate among people right now, in the place where you live and the area you are studying, are also influenced by the same archetypal patterns that give myths their energy and give shape to our collective sense of history. Sometimes those influences are subtle, while at other times they are obvious; in all cases, taking them into account will give you a clearer sense of the landscape of stories that surrounds you in your research. Think of the current stories circulating in the area you are

studying as legends of the present and you can sense something of their potential importance.

2. Many of these legends of the present belong to a category that has its own name in modern folklore studies: "urban legends." This is not a very useful term, since rural areas are at least as well stocked with legends of the present as urban neighborhoods are, but it has become widespread in recent years and plenty of books and websites use the phrase as a convenient label. You can use it to search for legends relevant to the area you are studying.

3. In the landscape of stories, legends of the present function differently from the histories, myths, and legends of the past we have already discussed. The key distinction is that legends of the present are usually much more subject to change than the other three categories of story. The difference here is like the difference between climate and weather: the climate of a region changes only very slowly by human standards, while the weather can veer around unpredictably in a matter of minutes. Legends of the present give you a way of measuring the current weather of consciousness.

4. Matters of location and geographical scale deserve just as much attention in studying legends of the present as they do with stories of other kinds. This is especially true nowadays, when the internet and other electronic communications media allow urban legends and other stories of the present to spread around the world in a matter of seconds. A story that appears and then vanishes may have nothing significant to do with the land and its mysteries; it may simply be a temporary ripple moving through the pool of humanity's collective consciousness, or a story relevant to some other place that happens to have spread a little further than usual.

5. Two signs highlight those legends of the present that are most relevant to earth mysteries research. The first is a connection to some local place or phenomenon. Even a legend as widespread as the familiar story of the hitchhiking ghost who is picked up by a driver on the anniversary of her death in a car accident becomes a matter of local legend if it is assigned to a particular spot on a road in your area, or some other specific place. The link to the landscape shows that in the minds of local people, the story resonates with a known location, and that offers important clues to the influences of the land at that place.

6. The second sign that marks a legend of the present as relevant to earth mysteries research is durability. Most stories of the present come and go with shifts in the collective thinking of humanity. When a story remains current in one place but disappears in other places, that difference is worth noting. Such a story, if it lasts long enough, may be on its way to a new role as a legend of the past or even as a myth. Whether or not this is the case, if it endures in the area you are studying, it has something to teach about the influences of that area.
7. Just as shifts in weather over time give warning of potential changes in climate, shifts in legends of the present can thus offer a glimpse into deeper changes in the collective consciousness of the region you are studying. Since those deeper changes unfold over time scales longer than any one human incarnation, it is unlikely that you will ever be able to know for certain which way consciousness is shifting. This is one of the ways in which the work of earth mysteries research necessarily unfolds over historical time. The contributions of earlier researchers may give you insights you would not otherwise have had, and your contributions in turn may provide the same help to students of earth mysteries in the future.

Practical work

During the week you spend on this lesson, pay special attention to the stories, rumors, and urban legends set in the present time that you may encounter. Consider reading a book or a few websites on urban legends to help guide your further explorations in the field.

Question for reflection

If the stories circulating in your community today survive for centuries, what might people in the far future make of them?

LESSON 31

Stories of beginnings

Seed thought

The assumption that man in his whole glory was created on the sixth day of Creation, without any preliminary stages, is after all somewhat too simple and archaic to satisfy us nowadays. There is pretty general agreement on that score. In regard to the psyche, however, the archaic conception holds on tenaciously.
—C. G. Jung, *Memories, Dreams, Reflections*

Orientation

1. Most people, even among those who know very little about mythology, have some sense that a great many myths describe the creation of the world. This is true, but it needs to be understood in a broader sense than it is usually given. Not all creation myths carry that label! Legends of beginnings very often make use of the same themes that shape the more obviously mythic stories of creation. Nor are historical narratives exempt from the same rule. Very often, the stories that are taught in schools about the birth of a country or

the founding of a city display, beneath a very thin layer of historical disguise, standard elements of creation myth.

2. It makes perfect sense that this should be the case. Stories, as pointed out in an earlier lesson, are the raw material from which each of us constructs an image of the world we inhabit. Stories are inevitably shaped by archetypes, the basic structures of human consciousness. In societies that take myths seriously, mythic narratives about the beginning of the world are given special importance, and are recited or read at certain special times. In societies like those of the modern industrial world, which think they have outgrown myths, legends and historical narratives fill the same role and end up being shaped by the same archetypes.

3. The influence of archetypes on supposedly factual narratives is often very marked. Anthropologist Misia Laudau, in her 1991 book *Narratives of Human Evolution*, reviewed standard accounts of human evolution from the nineteenth and twentieth century, and showed that every one of them followed the exact plot of a traditional hero tale, with all the incidents named by Joseph Campbell and other scholars of mythology. That was no accident. Human beings think with archetypes as inevitably as they walk with feet and eat with mouths, and every story human beings tell about their own beginnings will thus end up being drawn into the same archetypal forms that guide the makers of myths.

4. The same patterns that shape stories of the beginning of the world also come into play whenever human beings tell stories about beginnings on a smaller scale. The discovery of a continent or an island, the arrival of settlers, the establishment of a nation, and the founding of a city can all function as covert creation myths. Notice what roles stories of these kinds play in community life in your area at present, and what roles they played in earlier times. This can help you determine which of these narratives have importance in the collective imagination of the region you are studying.

5. Other, more specific beginnings are also worth studying in this context. What are your local industries and important businesses, and are stories about their founding important in the community? Are certain buildings especially important as centers of local pride or embarrassment, and are stories about their construction still in circulation? Collect those stories and see what they have to say to you.

6. To make sense of stories of beginnings, it is often helpful to start with a good general knowledge of creation myths in general. It very often happens that images found in explicit creation myths in one part of the world appear in recognizable form in stories of beginnings elsewhere that masquerade as legend or history. Very often, too, the themes that are central to the disguised creation myths of a region are those that play no part in the stories that talk in overtly mythic terms about the beginning of things.
7. If you know how and why a thing came into being, you understand something crucial about it. If you know how and why other people believe a thing came into being, you understand something crucial about *them*. The stories about beginnings that are common in the area you are studying, or that used to be common there, can give you important glimpses into the character of the land and the way that the people who live there respond to it. Combine those glimpses with the evidence of other stories more directly relevant to earth mysteries studies and you can begin to glimpse the shape of the landscape of narratives that once gave old sacred sites their meaning.

Practical work

During the week you spend on this lesson, sort through the stories you have gathered and see how many of them can be understood as overt or covert creation myths. Make a special effort to locate as many stories of beginnings as you can from your area; include religious teachings about Creation, scientific accounts of prehistory, historians' descriptions of the settlement of the area and the birth of the nation to which it belongs, and so on. See what these stories have in common and what differences separate them.

Question for reflection

Consider your own beginning and the beginnings of the things in your life that are important to you. What stories do those beginnings tell?

LESSON 32

Stories of mysterious places

Seed thought

The oddly crowded stones, the erosions of the oolitic limestone and their peculiar relationship have given rise to legends. The story is one of baffled ambition and guardian witchcraft. An ambitious local king (unnamed) is assured of ruling all England if from the Rollright site he can see Long Compton. Coming along with his men to fulfill this simple requirement, he found that Mother Shipton (surrogate for a witch of any kind) had caused the ground to rise in the manner it now does and so prevented the view.

—Ross Nichols, *The Book of Druidry*

Orientation

1. The realms of myth, legend, and history overlap in many ways with the physical landscape. In most parts of the world, the most important physical features of the land figure largely in the stories told nearby, whether those stories take the form of myths, legends, or historical accounts. For the student of earth mysteries, however,

the two landscapes come closest together when stories have gathered around ancient sites.

2. The example in the seed thought for this lesson is as typical as any such legend can be. The Rollright Stones are a stone circle in Oxfordshire, England, built in Neolithic times. Traditionally no one can count the stones and get the same figure twice. The local legend has it that the stones were once the king and his men, who had been transformed by Mother Shipton's magic, and an ancient elder tree standing nearby was the witch herself, still keeping watch. At midnight, the spell lifts briefly, and the stones go down to the nearby stream to drink.

3. Many other stone circles have similar stories, but it is rare to find any two that are identical. In the same way, other ancient sites scattered across the landscape have collected stories of their own; here, too, they often fall into similar categories by type, but the details almost always vary from one example to another. This pattern of general similarities balanced by local variations is useful for the student of earth mysteries. Learn the general pattern and you can recognize broad patterns in human consciousness; pay attention to the specific form the story takes in your area, and this can point you toward intriguing discoveries.

4. One of the great discoveries of folklore studies in recent decades is just how long folk memory can endure. Researchers have found, for example, that people in several parts of the world have folktales that preserve accurate details of the shape of sea coasts before the oceans rose at the end of the last ice age some 11,000 years ago. A folktale attached to an ancient site is entirely capable of preserving, in fragmentary form, some dim memory of political events or religious traditions dating back millennia.

5. The Rollright story, to return to the example above, may thus retain a folk memory of a political crisis of the Bronze Age: one of the burial mounds near the Rollright circle, say, might commemorate a local king whose pursuit of a larger realm was cut short by sudden death. Equally, certain archaic myths tell of gods or rulers who presided over an age of the world and then died or vanished; the legends of King Arthur very likely echo a myth of this kind, which got attached to the great war leader of post-Roman Britain in folktales, and the Rollright story may be the last faint echo of another such story.

6. It is rarely possible to pick out the historical or mythological basis of a story of this kind, if it dates back far enough. With tales of more recent vintage, clustering around people who are sufficiently well documented in the historical record, clarity can be easier to find, but even fairly recent stories can resist analysis. This is when paying attention to fine details comes into its own. If a direction is named in the story, like the sightline from the stones to Long Compton, what lies in that direction? What stars rise there at important seasons of the year, or what site of legendary importance can be found there?
7. In gathering stories about mysterious places, finally, do not neglect the stories being told by other earth mysteries researchers. Modern accounts of ancient sites are, among other things, another category of legends of the present, and are worth your attention even if you decide that they are factually inaccurate. Like the physical landscape, the landscape as it is remembered in narrative form is always changing, and stories about mysterious places that are in circulation today can give you a glimpse of the meaning that those places will have to people in the future.

Practical work

By now you will probably have collected as many stories about the mysterious sites in your area as you can find. If not, during the week you spend on this lesson, go looking for stories of this kind and see what you can locate. If you already have a good collection, review them and think about what they might have to tell you.

Question for reflection

What stories might people in the far future tell about the ruined remnants of our age?

LESSON 33

Stories of mysterious events

Seed thought

The subjects which we are trying to study have been taboo for generations and are only just now beginning to be taken seriously by the scientific world. The majority of scientists today, by reason of the long training they have had in other branches of study, are less likely to be able to adapt themselves to the new ideas than persons who have not been so extensively trained. It is probable that, as with most subjects at an early stage of their development, the big discoveries will be made by laymen.
—T. C. Lethbridge, *Ghost and Ghoul*

Orientation

1. When strange things happen, people very often tell stories about them. If the strange events are striking enough, or if they are repeated, those stories very often become part of the enduring narrative heritage of the area. No matter how improbable the resulting stories may seem, it is worth considering the possibility that they are rooted in paranormal experiences that people have had at various points in the past.

2. It is in stories of strange events that the lines between myth, legend, and history are hardest to draw. Many historical accounts of events in the past, as mentioned earlier, contain lightly concealed mythic themes, just as many myths contain details recalled from the historical past, and legends routinely blend the historical and archetypal at every turn. Add paranormal happenings to this mix and the line between the Seen and the Unseen cam become exceptionally difficult to draw.
3. With stories of strange events, as a result, it can be even more difficult than usual to tease out the actual events from the archetypal material. It is not enough to compare such stories to their equivalents in distant places and times, and treat anything that recurs frequently as an archetype. After all, strange as they appear to us, paranormal events do seem to fall into certain stable categories that are reported reliably in most if not all parts of the world, and people in many other cultures treat them as ordinary events of everyday life.
4. Many folklore scholars assume that paranormal events do not happen, and therefore any account of strange phenomena in folklore must have been inspired by older accounts in legend and myth. This does sometimes happen, of course. As we will see in a later lesson, many accounts of unknown lights or objects seen in the sky have been powerfully influenced by the widespread popular conception that such things must be spacecraft from another planet. In these and other cases, details that fail to match up with accepted narratives routinely get left out, while other details are interpolated as the story passes from person to person.
5. It also happens, however, that certain paranormal events described in folklore are also being experienced by people here and now. In his book *The Terror That Comes in the Night*, for example, researcher David Hufford started out researching a folktale theme about a particular class of nocturnal haunting, and discovered to his astonishment that many people reported having experiences identical to the folktale. As he pursued his investigation further, he discovered that the experience was just as common in people who had never heard of the folktale as it was in those who knew about it.
6. One of the consequences of modern industrial society's rejection of the Unseen is that very often, people who have witnessed strange events never talk about their experiences, and have no idea that many others have had similar encounters. As Hufford found, it is

entirely possible for an experience to be very common, even though nobody talks about it and nobody who has had it knows that anyone else has had it. In such cases a handful of local stories may provide the clue that allows an investigator to unravel a remarkable pattern of paranormal occurrences.
7. In examining stories of strange happenings, therefore, it is always helpful to watch for details that appear more than once in local tales, or can be found in recent paranormal accounts. An open mind is even more important here than elsewhere in earth mysteries research, since any given theme in a narrative of the paranormal may have come from the media, from other stories, from archetypal sources deep within the mind, or from actual experience. Patience and a willingness to follow the data wherever it leads are essential.

Practical work

During the week you spend on this lesson, review the legends you have gathered, looking for accounts of strange and paranormal events in the area you are studying. See if you can connect the legends with more recently reported paranormal happenings, including events you yourself have witnessed or investigated.

Question for reflection

What experiences have you had that you have never described to anyone else?

LESSON 34

Stories of the future

Seed thought

Whenever a civilization approaches a dramatic turning point, some symbol or concept arises to crystallize that change. The shining eagle of the Roman Legions, the Templars' cross on the sails of the Conquistadores, have been such symbols, spelling the end of one world and the dawn of another. For the world of the coming decades, the key symbol may be a shining disk from heaven.

—Jacques Vallee, *Messengers of Deception*

Orientation

1. Not all myths and legends recount events in the past or the present. Some predict happenings in the future. The Norse narrative of Ragnarok, the Twilight of the Gods, is an example many people know about. The events of the gods' final battle against the frost giants and other evil beings are described in detail in the *Elder Edda*, even though those events had not yet happened when those stories were originally told, and they have not happened yet.

2. Most cultures, ours very much included, have similar stories that anticipate what everyone expects to happen in the future. Whether these stories turn out to be correct or not is less important than what they have to say about the people who believe them and the land in which they are believed. Understand what people in a region think the future holds for them and you have a crucial source of information about how they imagine the land and themselves.
3. Cultures vary in the degree to which stories about the future interest them. On one end of the spectrum are societies in which most people believe the world has settled into an enduring state and will never change in any way that matters. On the other end are societies obsessed with some specific narrative about the future, in which most people wait impatiently for the long-predicted future to appear. Most societies fall somewhere in the middle; ours, by contrast, are among the most future-obsessed societies on record.
4. The industrial societies of the modern Western world are also unusual in that they are obsessed with two competing narratives about the future. On the one hand is the narrative of progress, which promises an endless onward march of ever-improving technology culminating in a gaudily imagined future in space. On the other is the narrative of apocalypse, which promises a sudden catastrophe that will flatten the proud towers of modern civilization. These two narratives are so deeply ingrained in the collective imagination of our time that many people are literally unable to imagine a future that does not conform to one or the other.
5. It can be enlightening to pay attention to the way that popular thinking moves from one of these competing narratives to the other, and to future predictions that blend the two narratives together—when, for example, progress is reinterpreted as leading to catastrophe, or catastrophe is reimagined as a door to progress. These offer a sensitive gauge of the hopes and fears of our time, and to the way those hopes and fears express themselves in different regions. These quite often conceal important clues to the subtle influence of the land.
6. It is also worth remembering that not all stories about the future are framed as predictions in any obvious way. Much of the modern folklore around the UFO phenomenon, for example, uses assorted ideas about alien life forms as a screen onto which hopes and fears about the future can be projected indirectly. Religious teachings that encourage their followers to focus on improving the world, or reject

the world and place their hopes on heaven, also embody stories about the future in an indirect way.
7. In an age of mass media saturated with predictions about what to expect in the future, it can be difficult to tease out local and regional stories about the future from the background of popular culture. Very often it is necessary to listen carefully to conversations and look into indirect stories of the sort described above to get some sense of what people actually expect from the future, as distinct from what they have been told they are supposed to expect. Since the future people have been told to expect by and large is not the one they get, attending to such things is among other things a good way to avoid being taken by surprise by events to come.

Practical work

During the week you spend on this lesson, look through your collection of local legends and stories and see how many of them are oriented to the future, directly or indirectly. See what these stories of the future tell you about the area you are studying and the people who live there.

Question for reflection

How would it affect you if the future turns out to be wholly unlike what you expect?

LESSON 35

Stories of the conventional wisdom

Seed thought

The passion for explanation—explanationism—is a peculiarly modern folly. We have come to expect explanations whenever anything mysterious occurs, and there is always an "expert" willing to oblige. No matter how ludicrous the expert's explanation, we are usually satisfied because we would rather be assured that the mystery has been solved than give it a moment's thought.
—Patrick Harpur, *Daimonic Reality: A Field Guide to the Otherworld*

Orientation

1. One further set of stories is usually neglected by students of legends and of earth mysteries generally. These stories are the ones told by scientists when they try to explain away mysterious sites, puzzling tales, and strange phenomena. Many people who are interested in earth mysteries tend to roll their eyes when such stories come to their attention, but this is a mistake. The stories of the conventional wisdom also have something to teach.

2. The UFO researchers of the twentieth century's middle decades had a useful term—"wipe"—for the arguments deployed by pseudoskeptics, the people who claim to be skeptics but whose claims depend on blind faith in the dogmatic beliefs of modern materialist science. Wipes might best be understood as legends of a certain peculiar kind. Like many other legends, they are about events that actually happened, but they redefine the people, places, and things involved in those events to remove every trace of enchantment from them. Where most legends are stories of enchantment, wipes are stories of disenchantment.
3. It is important to realize that not all wipes are inaccurate. It does happen sometimes that a seemingly mysterious light in the sky turns out to have a perfectly ordinary explanation. Hoaxes do take place now and then, and people do occasionally mistake the results of alcohol, psychedelic drugs, or mental illness for genuine mysterious phenomena. Students of earth mysteries need to be aware of these possibilities.
4. At the same time, an origin of the sort just described does not necessarily make a story of strange happenings irrelevant. For a hallucination, a hoax, or a case of mistaken identity to become a widely circulated story in a region, something in the character of that region must resonate with the thing that the witnesses thought they saw. Enchantments are well known to make things look like what they are not!
5. The problem with wipes, and with the whole range of stories that support the conventional wisdom in the face of all evidence to the contrary, is that they try to force the complex patterns of human experience into the rigid straitjacket of modern materialist dogma. Paradoxically, this also makes them useful to the earth mysteries researcher, because the stories told by pseudoskeptics and other defenders of the conventional wisdom are just as much a part of the body of local legend as any other story. They often draw just as deeply on archetypes and mythic patterns as the phenomena they try to explain away.
5. In interpreting the stories of the conventional wisdom, then, it is often necessary to treat them as you would a myth or a legend, to look for archetypal patterns at work, and to compare the wipes common in a given region with one another and with comparable wipes in other areas. The same kind of thinking that allows mythic images

to be recognized in history and urban legend is just as helpful for spotting the same deep structures in the narratives circulated by the defenders of the cultural mainstream.
6. When your local self-proclaimed skeptics try to blame every unusual event on pranksters, for example, it's often worth considering the possibility that this is how the archetype of the Trickster is taking shape in the present day. Equally, when the skeptics insist that everyone who saw something they don't consider real must have been drunk, hallucinating, or unbalanced, this might best be seen as an expression of the mythic rivalry behind Apollo and Dionysus.
7. Stories are the raw material of human knowledge, and so the stories told by people who insist they don't believe in stories are as significant as any other tale. This is especially true when the tales such people tell are as elaborate and imaginative as the most lively legend, as of course they so often are. Recognize wipes as legends, assembling the raw material of real or assumed events into patterns derived from archetypal sources, and they can provide unexpected insights into the way human consciousness deals with the influences of the land.

Practical work

During the week you spend on this lesson, locate and read as many wipes as you can concerning the mysterious places, stories, and phenomena of the area you are studying. Include the obviously absurd examples as well as those that are apparently sensible. Notice any common themes, especially themes that appear in wipes that attempt to dismiss a range of different unexplained events.

Question for reflection

What stories are the wipes you have encountered trying to tell, and what do those stories have to teach you?

LESSON 36

The narrative landscape

Seed thought

The dowser's rod twitches as he crosses the spot where once an old stone marked the corner of a subterranean rift. The sensitive person feels the magnetic surge within the stone ring. For such places still bear the invisible mark of some feat of natural magic, performed by the adepts of the former world, space and time travelers, masters of revelation, to whom the earth was but another living creature, responding like a man to certain shapes, sounds and poetic correspondences, the keys to universal enlightenment.
—John Michell, *The View Over Atlantis*

Orientation

1. The points made in previous lessons can be summed up in a single concept, simple but far-reaching: the concept of the *narrative landscape*. Just as there is a physical landscape underlying every human community and region, a structure of hills, valleys, plains, mountains, or whatever the local landforms happen to be, there is also a narrative

landscape that underlies the same community and region: a structure of histories, myths, and legends woven into the landforms, which orients the inhabitants to the physical landscape and gives human meaning to the landforms that surround them.

2. Anyone who has moved to an unfamiliar area and remained there long enough to learn the local geography and culture knows something about narrative landscapes. Among the things that every newcomer must learn to become oriented to a new community are the meanings the local culture gives to places: what social status the different neighborhoods have, where the important annual events take place, and so on. With time and careful listening, the newcomer begins to pick up memories and stories that define the land in the minds of its residents. These are important parts of the narrative landscape.

3. The narrative landscape goes deeper than the memories of current residents, however. It includes echoes of bygone events, some of them reaching far back into the past. This deeper layer of the narrative landscape can show itself in unexpected ways. Notice, for example, how often imaginative fiction from England uses Celtic themes to hint at antiquity: a good example is the elves of J. R. R. Tolkien's novels, who speak a language modeled on Welsh. Fifteen centuries after the Celtic peoples of what is now England were displaced or absorbed by Saxon invaders, their culture remains a living factor in the narrative landscape.

4. To help get a sense of how the narrative landscape functions, imagine a map of the area you are studying. On the map, in place of the usual markings, are written all the stories that have ever been told about places in the area—stories from history, from myth, and from legend. Some of those stories have been forgotten, and only dim traces of the writing can still be read. Others are alive in the local memory, and are written clearly.

5. Some local geographical features that are very prominent in other maps may hardly be noticed in this map of the narrative landscape, while other places less obviously important have become prominent because of the things that have happened there. When history, myth, and legend all cluster around a single place, as at certain ancient sites such as Stonehenge, that place stands out in a way that demands close attention. In other places, the narrative landscape may be very thin, or it may have been erased in various ways.

6. It can be useful as well as entertaining to create a map of the kind just described. This is best done once you have a good collection of local histories, myths, and legends from the area you are studying, and know the area well enough that you can place the narratives accurately on the map. The outlines need not be mathematically correct—if one part of your area has many more stories associated with it than others, make that part of the map larger so you have room for the stories. Write in as much detail as needed to identify the story. If you like, include little drawings showing landscape features and sites, or recalling details of a story.
7. Those who grew up with fantasy novels that included maps of imaginary countries know how such maps can contribute to a sense of enchantment. In a very real sense, the sort of map you are encouraged to draw this week is a map of an imaginary country, too—a country shaped and vitalized by the collective imagination of the people who live there. All countries are imaginary because the imagination plays so important a role in the human experience of the land. Let this awareness guide your study and work during this week.

Practical work

During the week you spend on this lesson, review the work you have done over the last three months exploring the stories that structure the area you are investigating. Notice common themes among the histories, myths, and legends you have collected, and notice also if there are any themes that have obviously been left out. Try to draw some tentative conclusions about the nature of the area and its interactions with human consciousness. While you are doing this, consider mapping out the narrative landscape of the area as explained above.

Question for reflection

What are the stories that tell you most about the region you are studying, and what do they say to you?

UNIT FOUR

PHENOMENA

LESSON 37

Overview of phenomena

Seed thought

Apparitions and the like are held to be impossible—if people claim to have seen funny things, then those people are deluded. The trouble is, if it is a delusion, it is one which has persisted throughout history and seems to be as prevalent now as it has ever been, to judge from the number of reported sightings of all kinds of anomalous entitles, from ghosts to "flying saucers" and mysterious big black cats, from lake monsters to Virgin Marys and weird "extraterrestrials."

—Patrick Harpur, *Daimonic Reality:*
A Field Guide to the Otherworld

Orientation

1. With this section we enter into the strangest dimension of earth mysteries research. It is one thing to study places where ancient peoples built structures whose purpose we no longer understand, or to collect stories about remarkable events in the distant or recent past. It is quite another to realize that ordinary people are encountering

strange phenomena here and now, in our supposedly modern, up-to-date, scientific world. The contemporary belief in the disenchantment of the world insists that events of this kind no longer happen—and yet they do.

2. It is of course true that some people like to make up stories about phenomena. It is equally true, however, that many people who have experienced phenomena rarely talk about them, for fear of what their friends and family will think. Every investigator into paranormal events has encountered witnesses who have to be coaxed gently into telling what they know, and are sure that nobody will believe them. In an age that insists the world must behave according to human ideas of rationality, there are many of these silent witnesses.

3. In making sense of phenomena, three basic principles are worth keeping in mind. The first is that many people do, in fact, encounter very strange things. Surveys carried out in many places have found that anything up to a third of the population has witnessed at least one thing that cannot be explained by the ideologies of modern materialist science. Such experiences are as common in well-educated people as they are in those who never finished high school, and in agnostics and people who simply aren't interested in spiritual things as they are in devout believers. They are an ordinary part of human life in every age.

4. The second principle is that there is an important difference between what people encounter and how they understand their experiences. The same cluster of bright lights seen moving through the air on a dark night might be interpreted as an alien spacecraft by a modern American, but it would have been interpreted as the terrible Wild Hunt chasing souls across the sky by a medieval German, and as a group of flying witches carrying lanterns by a member of certain East African tribes in the recent past. Whether or not these explanations are correct is one question. Whether the lights themselves existed is another.

5. The third principle is that very often, phenomena of the sort we are discussing have a close association with places. This is the factor that brings them into the field of earth mysteries. During the heyday of the UFO phenomenon, researchers noted that unexplained lights in the sky tended to concentrate in certain places, which came to be called "windows." This same discovery has been made many times before. Some phenomena, such as hauntings, occur in very specific

places; others, such as flying lights, appear in regions up to 200 miles across. Some relation to place, however, is extremely common.
6. In many cases, this connection between phenomena and place brings in one or both of the other subjects of earth mysteries research we have discussed already. Some ancient sites have phenomena associated with them. Many stories record the encounters between people in past times and phenomena like the ones witnesses face today. Some of the most intriguing of all earth mysteries include sites, stories, and phenomena in a single intricate fabric of human experience. You may or may not have the chance to research such a mystery, but it is well to know that the possibility is there.
7. Many researchers into earth mysteries have suggested that one reason ancient sites are placed where they are is that phenomena have occurred there, and one reason why myths and legends stay vivid in the popular mind is that they record phenomena that appear from time to time. A good deal of evidence supports this view. In dealing with phenomena, then, you are approaching the wellspring of earth mysteries, the set of experiences in which human beings draw closest to the enchantment in the land.

Practical work

During the week you spend on this lesson, begin compiling a list of the strange phenomena that have occurred in your area if you have not already started to do so. Depending on how famous the local phenomena happen to be, this might be an easy process or a more difficult one. Talking to people you know can be helpful, though you will often get better results if you treat it as a matter of gathering stories and folklore. Whenever possible, find out the exact place and time in which the phenomenon took place.

Question for reflection

What things do you consider to be genuinely impossible?

LESSON 38

The phantasmagoria factor

Seed thought

Paranormal phenomena are so widespread, so diversified, and so sporadic yet so persistent that separating and studying any single element is not only a waste of time but will automatically lead to the development of a belief. Once you have established a belief, the phenomenon adjusts its manifestations to support that belief and thereby escalate it.
—John Keel, *The Mothman Prophecies*

Orientation

1. The human mind likes to fit the things it experiences into familiar categories. Most of the time this habit of ours is harmless, and in some situations it can be very helpful. A healer trying to understand a patient's illness, an architect figuring out the best way to roof a building, an earth mysteries researcher walking up to an ancient standing stone—all these, and many other people, depend on being able to say, "This belongs in the same category as these other things,

and what worked there will work here." Yet there are other situations where the same habit becomes a potent source of misunderstanding.

2. "The map is not the territory." This rule, proposed by the linguist Alfred Korzybski more than a century ago, should be kept in mind by every student of earth mysteries. The "territory," in this metaphor, is the raw material of earth mysteries research, the sites, stories, and phenomena that we explore and try to interpret. The "map" is the set of theories, categories, and other mental constructs we use in our attempt to make sense of the data. As mentioned in the previous lesson, there is often a very great difference between the things people experience and the ways they interpret their experiences. The first of these is the territory, the second the map.

3. Research into unexplained phenomena is particularly subject to confusion between these things for at least two reasons. The first is that these phenomena challenge some of the most basic assumptions our culture makes about what reality is. To face such a challenge is always stressful. One very common way to deal with that stress is to flee into some other set of assumptions about reality, even though these may fit the phenomena just as poorly as the original set. It has happened far too often that researchers into strange phenomena have become just as dogmatic about the things they study as the mainstream scientists they oppose—the dogma is different but the attitude is the same.

4. The second reason why confusion between map and territory is so common in these studies is hinted at in the seed thought for this lesson. The phenomena we study spill over into the realms of mind and consciousness. This means that we are trying to perceive these things with the same inner capacities we use to try to understand them—and in this way our assumptions about what we are studying can influence what we perceive. Even in less elusive situations, we often notice the things that support our beliefs and miss those that conflict with them. When the mind is more directly involved in perception, this is even more of a problem.

5. Our minds are not the only source of this confusion, however. Many researchers into the unexplained have noticed that the phenomena themselves seem to adjust to our beliefs and our expectations. This implies that the phenomenon, or some other reality hidden behind them, is intelligent and aware of the work of researchers—and the evidence suggests that in at least some cases, the phenomena or the hidden reality behind them are more intelligent than we are.

6. Thus it is crucial in any research into phenomena to keep the kind of open mind discussed in earlier lessons—to accept nothing and reject nothing, to refuse to embrace any one explanation for what witnesses have seen, and above all, to include everything that witnesses report—or that you yourself experience!—whether or not it fits some set of categories or type of explanations. If flying lights of the UFO variety are sighted above a particular town, in other words, don't ignore the witnesses who report seeing a hairy humanoid of the "skunk ape" variety on the outskirts of the same town, or the ghostly black dog who was seen pacing across the road by the churchyard a mile away on the same evening.
7. The word "phantasmagoria"—literally "a gathering of phantoms"—was coined many centuries ago as a label for situations in which many different strange phenomena were all active at once. In a very real sense, the world we live in is a phantasmagoria. In researching strange events associated with the land, it is important to keep this in mind, and to be aware of the possibility that seemingly unrelated phenomena may all be related in some way, whether we can understand the connections or not.

Practical work

Take some time to think about the assumptions you have about different kinds of strange phenomena. What do you think UFOs really are? What do you think hairy humanoids like Bigfoot really are? What about ghosts? Think about the possibility that these things and other strange phenomena may actually be something very different from your expectations. You do not need to make up your mind about these things, and in fact it is more helpful if you do not. Just let yourself reflect on your own assumptions and expectations. Such reflections will make it a little easier for you to notice when these are distorting your awareness.

Question for reflection

What explanations for strange phenomena do you find most and least appealing?

LESSON 39

Ghosts and hauntings

Seed thought

You often hear people remark, "If I saw a ghost, I think I should die of fright." This is not the case at all. On two occasions I have clearly seen figures of people who were not really there, in the ordinary sense, at all. On neither occasion did I appreciate till later that there was anything strange in what I had seen.
—T. C. Lethbridge, *Ghost and Ghoul*

Orientation

1. Few if any paranormal events are more familiar to people nowadays, or more easily understood, than the appearances of ghosts. Folk beliefs and religious traditions in nearly every part of the world include the ideas that the human soul is capable of surviving the death of the body, and that under some circumstances the souls of the dead can appear to the living. Many people in today's industrial societies—up to a quarter, according to some surveys—believe that they have encountered at least one ghost. If you can get people

talking about their experiences, you will very often have an abundance of ghost lore to deal with.
2. The difficulty is usually getting people to talk. Two centuries or so of bullying by dogmatic materialists, who are quick to accuse anyone of lying or worse if they admit to encountering a ghost, has raised formidable barriers in the way of more openminded researchers. It is far from rare to discover that everyone in a large family or an entire neighborhood has witnessed a ghost or some other strange phenomenon, but none of them has ever talked about it with any of the others for fear of being dismissed as crazy.
3. Now that ghost hunting has become a recognized hobby with a substantial presence on the internet and in reality television, situations of this kind are becoming a little less common. If you investigate a haunting, make sure potential witnesses know that you are aware that ghosts exist and are interested in any local encounters with them. Very often that and a certain amount of ordinary courtesy and sympathy are all you will need to obtain detailed accounts. Many witnesses of ghostly phenomena are eager to talk about what they saw, so long as they know that they will not face bullying and ridicule.
4. In making sense of ghosts and hauntings, it is important to know that not all hauntings are the same. Researchers have divided the phenomena in various ways, which can be looked up in books on ghost investigation. For the researcher, the detail to keep in mind is that each haunting needs to be understood and investigated on its own terms. Each haunting is the product of a complex human situation in the past, and the experiences that witnesses report will vary just as much as those of an encounter with people who happen to be living.
5. One kind of haunting that deserves specific attention here is the poltergeist. This is a German word meaning "noisy ghost." A haunting counts as a poltergeist if it affects the material plane directly—for example, if objects are moved without being touched by anyone or any material thing, or if loud knocks or raps come from inside the walls when no material force could have caused that to happen. Poltergeists are among the most colorful forms of haunting and have attracted much attention from investigators.
6. Not all poltergeist phenomena are produced by ghosts. Most kinds of paranormal events and entities can become the focus of a poltergeist outbreak. Many investigators have noticed that poltergeist

phenomena can also happen around human beings who are frustrated in various ways and who unintentionally radiate their misery and anger in the form of subtle influences. If you have the chance to investigate an active poltergeist haunting, and a person who fits that description is also present, keep that possibility in mind.*

7. While you are collecting information about a local ghost or haunting, be sure to include in your studies any attempts that might be made to explain them away. In some cases the wipes being proposed by rationalists may be accurate—it does happen, for example, that ordinary natural phenomena may be mistaken for a ghost, and fraud and fakery also occur from time to time. Whether or not such claims are accurate, they are part of the human reaction to the phenomenon you are investigating, and can often tell you something about the collective thinking of your area and the way it relates to the stranger aspects of the land.

Practical work

During the week you spend on this lesson, read at least one book on ghosts in general, and also locate as many accounts of ghosts and hauntings in your area as you can. Compare them to accounts of ghosts and hauntings from other places, and see if there are any distinctive patterns in the local lore. Pay particular attention to hauntings that take place near sites that are of interest for other reasons.

Question for reflection

Do you believe in ghosts? Why or why not?

---

*It is rarely a good idea to talk about this to the people involved, however, unless they are already aware of the possibility. The tangled family psychology so often involved in this type of poltergeist haunting is best left to competent psychotherapists.

LESSON 40

Mysterious animals

Seed thought

It is true that black dogs, for instance, haunt particular stretches or road, certain lakesides, specific woods in a manner analogous to UFO and fairy preference for certain sacred sites. (The predilection of these to be linked by straight lines—"fairy paths," lung-mei or Chinese "dragon paths," and "leys"—has been documented by students of so-called earth mysteries.)
—Patrick Harpur, *Daimonic Reality: A Field Guide to the Otherworld*

Orientation

1. Even today, after more than three centuries of scientific investigation into the animal kingdom, new species are still being discovered, and familiar species are still being encountered in places where they were not known to appear. Those who have tracked living things in today's urbanized world know just how elusive and wary of human contact animals can be. Thus it should not come as a surprise that

people routinely report sightings of animals that, at least in theory, have no business being in the places where they are seen.
2. Considerations of this kind have given rise to the science of cryptozoology, the study of animals not yet known to science. Founded and named by the Belgian biologist Bernard Heuvelmans, cryptozoology is as rational as a science can be. The only thing that distinguishes it from other branches of biology is that it gathers evidence for the existence of living things not yet formally recognized by science. The fact that it is generally dismissed as pseudoscience by scientists unfamiliar with its findings shows, to an embarrassing degree, the roles that prejudice and fashion play in the supposedly objective judgments of the scientific community.
3. Cryptozoologists have collected extensive evidence for the existence of some animals not yet known to science, and intriguing clues pointing to the possible existence of others. Their work is valuable and deserves far more support and respect than it receives. Not all reports of unexpected or unknown animals, however, make sense in cryptozoological terms. Alongside reports of unknown or out-of-place animals are encounters with creatures that have animal forms, but seem instead to belong to the realm of phantoms and ghosts.
4. The legendary black dogs of England's west country are a case in point. Immortalized by Arthur Conan Doyle in the classic Sherlock Holmes novel *The Hound of the Baskervilles*, they are still frequently sighted in various corners of rural southwest England. Each appears in a familiar place, often on one of the old straight roads leading to a certain church; each one has a distinctive appearance, though glowing red eyes are common; local folklore often considers their appearance as an omen of death. They belong clearly enough to the lore of phantoms, not that of the unknown animals studied by cryptozoologists.
5. Other creatures lie closer to the poorly defined border between phantom and unknown animal. The "ABCs" (anomalous black cats) of Britain are a good example. They are large cats, resembling nothing so much as black panthers, which are sighted and occasionally photographed in various corners of rural Britain, where no such animal is known to live. Are they panthers, brought to the country as pets by some rich eccentric, that escaped from captivity? Are they some previously unknown species of felid, perhaps driven

from their mountain habitats by the encroachments of civilization? Are they phantoms pure and simple? Nobody knows.
6. Thus the boundary between cryptozoology and stranger phenomena can be very hard to trace. As a student of earth mysteries, your field of study embraces both ends of the spectrum of the unexplained, and it is usually unnecessary for you to decide in advance whether the black panther or the very strange bird sighted by your neighbors was a living creature unknown to science or a phantasm with no material body at all. If the evidence points one way or another, follow where it leads, but never close the door on the possibility that the creature you are investigating may not be what you expect.
7. It is always important to treat local legends and folklore about mysterious animals as a source of information. Sometimes these will turn out to be quite accurate, while in other cases the gap between legend and reality can teach you something about the collective thinking of the area, and thus about the character of the land. Always remember to include in your study the stories invented and circulated by skeptics to explain away sightings of mysterious animals. These are also folklore, as noted earlier; now and again they turn out to be correct, while the rest of the time they can offer helpful clues into the subconscious drives and dilemmas of the people who believe in them.

Practical work

During the week you spend on this lesson, sort out accounts of mysterious non-humanoid animals from the other material you have gathered. Decide, if you can, which of them are more likely to be living animals and which are more likely to be phantoms. Notice whether they are associated with other strange phenomena, with important local stories, or with ancient sites. Whether or not you have been able to gather any such material, read at least one book on mysterious animals.

Question for reflection

If you encountered the local mysterious or phantom animals in a dream or a scrying vision, what might they mean to you?

LESSON 41

Mysterious hominids

Seed thought

Far beyond North America, most cultures in other parts of the world also have ancient legends about hairy man-monsters often endowed with supernatural powers or amazing strength. Sometimes they are feared as man-eaters, and in other circumstances are merely left alone as much as possible. Occasionally these hairy ones have a place in tribal culture stories as heroes. In Native American lore, they often command a special respect and are thought of as a different kind of people rather than as animals.

—Linda S. Godfrey, *American Monsters*

Orientation

1. The same question that bedevils research into mysterious animals comes up with equal force in studying the apparently hominid or apelike mystery creatures reported in many corners of the world—BHMs ("big hairy monsters") in the jargon of today's investigators of the unknown. Humanlike creatures, generally bipedal and furry,

are routinely sighted in a great many places. Are they a species of primate not yet known to scientists, or are they phantasms connected with the stranger, more paranormal dimension of human experience? There are good arguments to be made for both claims.

2. Cryptozoologists have pointed out, for example, that a nine-foot-tall, heavily furred bipedal ape, known to scientists as *Gigantopithecus*, lived in northern and eastern Asia just a few million years ago. It would be perfectly plausible that one relict population of these creatures might have survived in the Himalayas, accounting for sightings of the Yeti or "abominable snowman," while another population could have crossed the Bering land bridge along with so many other animals and left descendants in isolated parts of the American West, giving rise to reports of Bigfoot and the Sasquatch.

3. Yet not all mysterious hominids, even furry ones, can be explained adequately by way of this strictly biological approach. Mysterious hominids of the Bigfoot type are routinely reported from urban or suburban areas in which no large wild primate could stay hidden for long, or find adequate food. Sightings of this sort quite often appear together with other paranormal events, such as mysterious lights seen in the sky. It is also unnervingly common for the tracks of mysterious hominids to end suddenly, as though the creature dissolved into thin air.

4. The great obstacle to clarity in these events, as in so many other mysterious happenings, is the insistence that all such events can have one and only one cause. It is entirely possible that small relict populations of *Gigantopithecus* survive in the mountains of East Asia and western North America; this does not mean that every hairy humanoid spotted anywhere on either continent must be a *Gigantopithecus*. Other factors and other beings—not all of them belonging to the material plane—can produce such sightings.

5. By and large, the differences between undiscovered animals and paranormal entities can be sorted out if it's kept in mind that animals by and large behave like animals, while beings from the Unseen behave in other ways. It is not necessarily hard to tell the difference between a large wild primate that avoids human beings and smells like a large unwashed animal, and a humanoid creature that goes out of its way to startle and harass human beings and has a sulfurous smell, like the devils of medieval folklore.

6. Local monster lore can be helpful in sorting out cryptozoological specimens from beings more likely to belong to the realm of the Unseen, but it has to be used with an eye out for mythic content. Many Native American legends, for example, portray animals who behave just like human beings, complete with tribal chieftains, medicine people, and social customs based on those of their Native neighbors. If local stories portray the Sasquatch or the skunk ape in similar terms, check to see if other stories do the same with bears, deer, and so on, before drawing sweeping conclusions.
7. Mysterious hominids, because they are so similar to human beings in some ways and so different in others, call up strong emotional reactions in us: even stronger, in many cases, than those evoked by other mysterious creatures. We see ourselves reflected in them, as in a fun house mirror. If the area you are studying has sightings or traditions about such creatures, see what they might have to say about how the people in the area think about themselves and the world around them.

Practical work

During the week you spend on this lesson, review any material you have found that relates to unknown humanlike creatures in your area. Notice whether they are associated with other strange phenomena, with important local stories, or with ancient sites. Whether or not you have been able to gather any such material, read at least one book on Bigfoot and similar beings.

Question for reflection

If the area where you live, or some area close by, turned out to be inhabited by an unknown primate, would that change the way you think about the land?

LESSON 42

Impossible creatures

Seed thought

In this book, I assemble some of the data that I think are of the falsely and arbitrarily excluded.
The data of the damned.
I have gone into the outer darkness of scientific and philosophical transactions and proceedings, ultra-respectable, but covered with the dust of disregard. I have descended into journalism. I have come back with the quasi-souls of lost data.
They will march.
—Charles Fort, *The Book of the Damned*

Orientation

1. In many cases, as noted in the last two lessons, it is hard to tell whether a sighting of a mysterious creature is best investigated by a cryptozoologist or a paranormal researcher. Some sightings, however, clearly belong all the way over on the paranormal side of the line. When an apparently physical entity appears out of thin air or disappears the same way, or when a creature appears to violate the

known laws of biology or physics, it becomes clear that zoologists, crypto- or otherwise, are out of their league.
2. Such sightings occur tolerably often. The Jersey Devil, one of the most famous homegrown American monsters, is one good example: with cloven hooves on its hind legs, batlike wings, a horselike head with horns, scaled skin, and glowing eyes and mouth, it cannot be assigned to any branch of the animal kingdom, and yet it has been sighted repeatedly and its hoofprints copied and measured. The *chupacabra* ("goat vampire" in Spanish) is a more recent paranormal creature, also seen by many people, which has glowing eyes, flies through the air despite lacking wings, and has the interesting habit of changing colors through the spectrum.
3. Any time witnesses experience something that violates the ordinary behavior of the material plane, it is worth exploring the possibility that the witnesses were in an altered mental state of some kind and perceived the realities of a different plane. As occultists know, this is not at all the same thing as saying the thing in question didn't happen! What UFO researcher Jenny Randles has termed "the Oz Factor"—the very common report of UFO witnesses that they seemed to enter another reality just before they observed something strange in the sky—should always be checked for.
4. Another issue worth keeping in mind is the influence of narratives on experiences. One famous chupacabra sighting in the early 1990s, for example, included pawprints in the farmyard where the creature had killed livestock. Photos of the pawprints showed clearly that the culprit was a large dog. In this case an urban legend rather than a paranormal creature was involved—though the legend is of interest to the student of earth mysteries in its own right, for reasons discussed in detail in Unit Three of this book.
5. Hoaxes are another possibility that has to be kept in mind, especially but not only in cases that seem to violate the known laws of nature. The more bizarre an event is, the more carefully it should be checked for evidence of fraud; most genuine paranormal events are relatively straightforward and fall into known categories, while hoaxers can rarely resist the temptation to go overboard with high strangeness.
6. Yet it does sometimes happen that creatures that cannot be explained by ordinary biology are witnessed by people who appear to be in ordinary states of consciousness and do not show any sign of being the product of narrative distortion or deliberate fraud. Such sightings

are notoriously difficult to explain in any way at all. It is only fair to point out, however, that no one ever promised our species that every event that happens should have an explanation that human beings can understand.

7. Whether they are the products of hoaxers, narrative influence, altered states of consciousness, or something very strange brushing against the edges of our reality, impossible creatures—like most unexplained phenomena—can be thought of as dream-images in the collective imagination of the time and place where they are seen. No matter what else an investigation into such creatures can or cannot do, close attention to the entity sighted as a symbol can help provide glimpses into the narrative landscape of the area you are studying.

Practical work

During the week you spend on this lesson, review any material you have gathered about impossible creatures in your area. Think of them as symbols from dreams or visions, and see if you can grasp some part of their meaning.

Question for reflection

How do you feel about the idea that the world contains creatures of the sort mentioned in this lesson?

LESSON 43

Appearances and disappearances

Seed thought

We shall pick up an existence by its frogs.

Wise men have tried other ways. They have tried to understand our state of being, by grasping at its stars, or its arts, or its economics. But, if there is an underlying oneness of all things, it does not matter where we begin, whether with stars, or laws of supply and demand, or frogs, or Napoleon Bonaparte. One measures a circle, beginning anywhere.

—Charles Fort, *Lo!*

Orientation

1. To proceed to this next category of paranormal phenomena is to complete our journey into the territory of the utterly bizarre. Most people can fit their minds around the existence of ghosts and unknown animals. But that material things might appear out of nowhere, or vanish into thin air—that is quite another matter. The one thing that ghosts, cryptids, and BHMs have in common with mysterious appearances and disappearances is that people witness them all.

2. It is hard to think of anything that seems more impossible, for example, than a shower of frogs falling from the sky. Charles Fort, that indefatigable investigator of the strange, collected 294 reports in newspapers and scientific journals of showers of living things, most often frogs and fish. There have been many more examples since his time. The excuse usually deployed by would-be skeptics—that a whirlwind must have scooped up the contents of a pond and dropped them somewhere else—will not work, because such falls are normally of a single species only. If frogs fall from the sky, the "whirlwind" somehow failed to pick up water plants, fish, muck, or anything else.
3. What could possibly cause a shower of frogs? Nobody knows. That simple fact represents the great challenge investigators face in dealing with mysterious appearances and disappearances. No reasonable theory to explain them has yet been offered. No known law of nature is able to explain them. All we know is that now and then, people witness the baffling spectacle of frogs, fish, or other things falling from the heavens—sometimes from a cloud, sometimes accompanied by rain, but sometimes simply plummeting out of a clear blue sky.
4. In the same way, things sometimes vanish without a trace, or show up without any ordinary way of arriving. So do people. No one knows how or why. In some cases like these it is hard to tell for certain if something paranormal has happened, for things and people very often have ordinary reasons for appearing or disappearing. In others, it is clear that something very strange has taken place. In still others, perfectly ordinary events have been taken up and transformed in the collective imagination to fit archetypal stories.
5. Because mysterious appearances and disappearances are relatively uncommon, it is very unlikely that you will have the opportunity to investigate an event of this kind while the evidence is still fresh. It is far more likely that you will be approaching a cold case, in which the only sources of evidence available to you are newspaper articles or personal recollections decades or centuries old. You may be going over ground that many previous investigators have already covered. Even if you happen to find a case that hasn't previously come to the attention of other researchers, your chance of finding anything unusual about it is fairly small.

6. That does not mean that cases of this sort are not worth investigating. It simply means that such cases are best approached with realistic expectations. If mysterious appearances and disappearances could be solved readily on the basis of the available evidence, they would not be mysterious any more. The data that you gather may guide you to small discoveries, and may someday help someone else take another step toward making sense of the mystery. That is more than enough to make these efforts worthwhile.
7. Mysterious appearances and disappearances sometimes seem to happen in isolation from other strange phenomena. In other cases, however, these events take place as part of a broader pattern of paranormal events, or in places that are marked out by ancient sacred sites or are the settings of narratives of various kinds. Here as elsewhere in earth mysteries research, it is always wise to place the subject of your study in context, and try to understand it in relation to the places and events that surround it.

Practical work

During the week you spend on this lesson, look for accounts of mysterious appearances and disappearances in the area you are studying. The books of Charles Fort are good resources for such accounts, but there are many others, and your research into local stories may have already brought examples of this kind to your attention. See if any of these events are associated with mysterious sites, or with other kinds of unexplained phenomena.

Question for reflection

Do you think that unexplained appearances and disappearances actually happen—and what sorts of evidence would it take to make you change your mind?

LESSON 44

UFOs 1 — Unraveling the confusion

Seed thought

But from the USA came strange reports. Lights in the sky, formerly dismissed as hallucinations or worse, were being reported with increasing frequency. Fears that they might be enemy secret weapons led to a spate of official government investigations, and a new popular name was coined—flying saucers.
—Nigel Pennick, *The Ancient Science of Geomancy*

Orientation

1. Of all the phenomena that appear in modern times to startle witnesses and perplex researchers into the unknown, unidentified flying objects—UFOs—are at once the most common and the most misunderstood. These days, if an unexplained light is seen moving across the sky, one set of true believers insists that it must be a spaceship from another world, while another set of true believers insists that if it wasn't some familiar object such as a planet or a passing plane, no one saw anything at all. It should be obvious that there are

many other possibilities. That this is not obvious is one of the strangest things about UFO phenomena.
2. The confusion has been made much worse than it has to be by a widespread habit, common to both of the camps just named, of ignoring or erasing details of sightings that fail to match up with their preconceptions. Accounts of famous sightings published in popular books very often differ drastically from the stories told by people who were there at the time, and the differences inevitably work to shore up one of the two belief systems just mentioned. In the process, a great deal of data—most of it remarkably strange—gets swept under the rug.
3. Straightforward reasons account for at least some of this confusion. From 1947 to the present, the US armed forces have been using "UFO sightings" as convenient camouflage for tests of secret aerospace technologies, and disinformation spread via networks of UFO believers has helped keep the camouflage in place. It is not an accident that UFOs so often looked like little silvery dots high in the air when the US was running secret tests of high-altitude balloons, or that UFOs shaped like black triangles were being seen while the US was testing the early prototypes of stealth aircraft. The governments of other nations have made ample use of this same convenient dodge as well.*
4. Alongside these deliberate deceptions, plenty of other less intentional sources of confusion have made the UFO phenomenon the tangled mess that it is. One of the most important of these is the power of narratives. Human beings normally use the stories they know to interpret the things they experience, even when the experiences have to be lopped and stretched considerably to fit the story. Once popular culture embraced the idea that UFOs must be alien spacecraft if they exist at all, that habit became a barrier in the way of understanding the phenomena surrounding UFOs.
5. If your research leads you to investigate a past or present UFO sighting, then, two basic rules need to be kept in mind. The first and most basic rule is to be aware of the possibility of fraud and deception, especially but not only if the information you have comes from a government or military source. There is a great deal of fakery in the UFO scene, and even more selective reporting and distortions of detail. If a sighting you are investigating happened some years ago,

---

*I have discussed this in detail in my book *The UFO Chronicles* (London: Aeon, 2020).

see if you can find accounts from as close as possible to the time of the sighting, and compare them to more recent accounts in the UFO literature. The differences can be remarkable.
6. The second rule is to take note of everything that happened, whether or not it fits any given hypothesis about what UFOs are or might be. If other strange phenomena happened in the same place and time, whether or not they have anything to do with lights in the sky, include them in your notes. This is especially important when they stray across the boundaries that most people use to sort out different categories of strange events: when lights in the sky appear in the same place as ancient standing stones, for example, or sightings of a BHM or other anomalous creature.
7. Whatever deeper connection may or may not exist between the lights and the megaliths, or the lights and the Sasquatch sightings, you can be sure of one thing: they took place on or above the same part of the earth's surface. That makes them clues to the unseen dimensions of that part of the land. This may not be as accidental as it seems. As we will see, strange phenomena tend to cluster in certain places, and the presence of more than one phenomenon can offer a valuable clue to the subtle dimension of that part of the land.

Practical work

During the week you spend on this lesson, find out what UFO sightings have occurred in your area. Gather as much information as you can about each sighting. Be careful to include the place or places from which the UFO was seen, and any sites, stories, and other phenomena that may be associated with the sighting.

Question for reflection

Have you or anyone you know seen a UFO—that is, an object in the sky you or the witness couldn't identify—and what do you think it was?

LESSON 45

UFOs 2—Earth lights

Seed thought

Our planet produces lights. A range of light phenomena emerges naturally from the Earth's own processes, but they are not fully understood. Some types of terrestrially produced lights, even though occurring fairly regularly and reported quite frequently and reliably, have barely been perceived by mainstream science or, more unexpectedly, by many of those people called "ufologists" whose self-appointed role is to study unexplained lights and aerial anomalies.

—Paul Devereux, *Earth Lights Revelation*

Orientation

1. One distinct presence that has been teased out of the phantasmagoria surrounding UFOs is a phenomenon that has come to be called "earth lights"—bright balls of light, often colored, which appear regularly in the sky in specific places. Britain's Pennine lights, the Marfa lights and Yakima lights in the United States, and the Hessdalen lights in Norway are among the most famous of these, but there are hundreds

of other areas where earth lights are seen. Today's scientists have no idea what they are or what causes them, and inevitably this causes many scientists to insist that they do not and cannot exist—yet people keep seeing them.
2. Several other light phenomena are sometimes confused with earth lights. Ball lightning is a rare phenomenon of thunderstorms; it takes the form of brilliant spheres of light which can "short out" when they hit a conductive object. Earthquake lights are light displays of various kinds that emanate from the earth before and during quakes. Swamp lights, also known as will o' the wisps and other folk names, are small, usually dim lights that hover in the air near swamps and marshes. None of these are adequately explained by current scientific knowledge, but all of them have been observed so often, by so many witnesses (including qualified scientists), that their reality is questioned only by dogmatic pseudoskeptics.
3. Earth lights differ from the three types just mentioned. They consist of basketball-sized glowing balls of light which appear in the same areas over a period of weeks, months, or many years. They are most often seen in regions where geological faults are under strain and electrically conductive minerals are close to the surface. They hover, move, change color and shape, and produce low humming, buzzing, or whistling sounds. In some cases they appear to respond to human action as though conscious. What are they? No one knows for certain.
4. One intriguing line of research carried out by investigators in recent decades focuses on the hypothesis that earth lights have a strong magnetic dimension. Geological faults can distort the earth's magnetic field, generating magnetic "hot spots." Strong magnetic fields have been shown to have strange effects on human consciousness. In medical jargon, these are described as dissociative states and vivid hallucinations; in the language of occultism and spirituality, the same states might better be described as trance states and visionary experiences opening onto other realms of being.
5. These magnetic "hot spots" were often identified as sacred places by the prophets and visionaries of ancient cultures, and those societies that used architecture to mark out sacred space very often built shrines, temples, stone circles, or other specialized structures on them. Earth lights sometimes appear in such places. As you research sites in your area, pay special attention to accounts of strange light

phenomena, no matter what form the lights may take. These may point to the presence of earth lights.

6. Human beings like to have explanations for the things they see, and earth lights and other unusual light phenomena are just as subject to this as anything else. Earth lights can be described in legend and folklore as angels from heaven, spirits carrying lamps, fiery dragons, lanterns on phantom ships or carriages, headlights on ghostly locomotives or automobiles, flying saucers from outer space, and much more. It takes practice and a careful eye to see through the details added by storytellers to recognize the presence of a mysterious light at the heart of it all.

7. If you have the opportunity to investigate earth lights and happen to see one, remember that you are dealing with an unknown form of energy that may or may not be safe to approach. Keep detailed notes on the experience, take photos or video if you can, but it may not be wise to approach the light. If your occult training has reached the stage at which you can communicate with spirits, on the other hand, speaking to the earth light is worth attempting, and might add considerably to knowledge of this strange phenomenon.

Practical work

During the week you spend on this lesson, sort through the data available to you to see if any of the anomalous events in your area seem to be associated with earth lights. If so, consider learning more about earth lights and applying that knowledge to your ongoing explorations. If any of the other forms of mysterious lights described above occur in your area, make a note of that as well.

Whether or not there are earth lights in your area, read up on this phenomenon in other parts of the world, using local libraries or the internet as resources.

Question for reflection

What do the abundant reports of earth lights witnessed by credible observers suggest to you about the nature of the world we live in?

LESSON 46

UFOs 3—The shamanic dimension

Seed thought

The real UFO story must encompass all of the many manifestations being observed. It is a story of ghosts and phantoms and strange mental aberrations; of an invisible world that surrounds and occasionally engulfs us; of prophets and prophecies, and gods and demons.

—John Keel, *Operation Trojan Horse*

Orientation

1. The place where evidence concerning the UFO phenomenon departs most sharply from the beliefs that try to confine it can be summed up very simply: many UFO encounters have remarkably close parallels to traditional shamanic teachings and experiences. It is clear that whatever is behind the mysterious lights in the skies, it has been going on for a very long time, and much of what is known about it can only be forced into the paired straitjackets of the extraterrestrial and rationalist belief systems by doing violence to the facts.

2. The word "shaman" comes from the Tungus language of central Siberia. It has been used by the Tungus and related Siberian peoples since time out of mind for their traditional healers and magicians, who gain their powers by entering into trance states and communing with beings that come from other realms of being. It is rare for people to choose to be shamans; instead, they have their powers thrust upon them unexpectedly by going through experiences in which they are contacted or abducted by otherworldly beings, receive teachings, undergo strange surgeries, and return to the human world with unusual psychic abilities.
3. In the eighteenth century, when the expanding Russian Empire came into contact with Siberian peoples who practiced shamanism, Western scholars began to study these traditions and noticed that many other tribal peoples around the world had similar teachings and practices. The late twentieth century saw another upsurge of interest in shamanism, and once again attention turned to the presence of shamanic themes in cultures across much of the world.
4. From this context it is not hard to recognize in UFO contactees and abductees, and in many other aspects of the broader UFO phenomenon, the familiar signs of shamanic experience. Like other shamans, people who believe they have been contacted or abducted by alien beings in UFOs have had the experience of being taken out of their ordinary lives in order to undergo strange experiences. Many of them show signs of having been in altered states of consciousness when they had their experience, along the line of the "Oz Factor" discussed in an earlier lesson. Many contactees and abductees, when they return to our world, discover that they have gained paranormal abilities of various kinds.
5. Just as shamanic experiences differ from shaman to shaman and from tribe to tribe, contactee and abductee experiences differ from person to person and from culture to culture. The common patterns of the experience are filled out with diverse details. In collecting and studying accounts of contactee and abductee experiences, close attention to the details is important. As with the other phenomena covered in this book, it is always worth watching to see whether mysterious places, local narratives, or other kinds of strange phenomena play any role in the local UFO legends.
6. More generally, UFO narratives in modern times have taken on many of the details of traditional myth and legend, lightly modified

to make them fit current intellectual fashions. Many people these days think they have stopped believing in gods, so when they think of superhuman beings in the sky, they picture those beings as extraterrestrials. The transformation of shamanic trances into UFO close encounters is among other things a good case study in how archetypal imagery has been retooled for modern times.
7. The psychologist Carl Jung, late in his life, wrote a short book entitled *Flying Saucers: A Modern Myth of Things Seen in the Sky*. In its pages he turned the same methods of analysis he used for patients' dreams on UFO reports, and described the entire UFO phenomenon as a collective waking dream with important lessons to communicate to the attentive observer. The same thing is true of all mysterious phenomena, on local as well as global scales. Approach local UFO sightings with this in mind and see what they have to teach you.

Practical work

During the week you spend on this lesson, read up on shamanism online or in your local library. With the information in mind, review any stories of personal encounters with UFO occupants you may have collected, and see whether and in what ways they correspond to shamanic experiences.

Question for reflection

Are there any aspects of UFO reports that remind you of other elements of traditional occult or spiritual lore, and if so, what aspects and what do they bring to mind?

LESSON 47

Flaps and windows

Seed thought

In this one small corner of Ireland it was obvious that well over half the population had either seen a specimen or knew of a sighting by some trusted member of their family. Yet this information was not transmitted. It had neither been investigated nor checked. For when a reliable observer did produce a written report and press it on the authorities, as Fr. Quigley did following his 1960 Ree sighting, this was merely tossed on a shelf and forgotten.

—F. W. Holiday, *The Dragon and the Disc*

Orientation

1. Paranormal phenomena are not smoothly distributed in space or time. Some places simply have more unexplained events than others, and those events tend to cluster in periods a few days or weeks or months in length, or take place at certain seasons or lunar phases, rather than occurring more or less at random. Researchers have found that if they pay attention to the clustering of strange events

in space and time, it often becomes possible to tease out unexpected insights from the phenomena.

2. UFO investigators have coined useful terms for these groupings. In UFO jargon, a burst of UFO sightings over a period of weeks or months is called a "flap," and a place where UFOs are seen much more often than elsewhere is a "window." Some investigators of the unexplained have come to use these same terms more generally for paranormal events of all kinds, since many other phenomena display similar patterns.

3. The size of a window can vary significantly from one type of paranormal event to another. Veteran paranormal researcher John Keel, for example, noticed that UFOs tended to cluster in areas around 200 miles across, and quite often traced out the same straight tracks across that region over and over again. At the other end of the spectrum, most hauntings are far more narrowly localized: tolerably often, for example, a ghost will be seen repeatedly in a single room of a haunted house, or a phantom black dog will appear on the same isolated stretch of country road.

4. In the same way, flaps vary both in length and in regularity. UFO flaps are routinely months long, for example, while mysterious creatures most often appear in a given area for a few days or weeks at most. In much the same way, mysterious appearances or disappearances that cluster in time tend to happen once and then never again occur in the same area, while it is very common for a haunting to repeat at regular intervals—for example, the ghost of a suicide may be seen every year on the anniversary of the death.

5. Among the most interesting aspects of flaps and windows is the tendency for different kinds of mysterious events to cluster in space and time. It is quite common for mystery animals or hominids to be seen at the same time that strange lights are spotted moving through the sky, or for baffling appearances or disappearances to be linked to a haunting or to some other form of uncanny event. This has suggested to many researchers that some single reality is behind many paranormal happenings.

6. For the student of earth mysteries, it is at least as important that paranormal events quite often cluster around mysterious sites. Close attention to local legends and folklore, and to events reported in recent times, will often reveal a long history of strange experiences connected with an ancient earthwork or a standing stone. This can

sometimes provide fascinating insights into what the site may have meant in ancient times.
7. It is also always worth checking to see if flaps follow some particular cycle in the calendar or the heavens, or whether windows seem to be oriented in any way to sites, perhaps even distant ones. Is the haunting only seen on the night of the full moon? Do the lights seen moving through the sky head in the direction of an ancient mound in the next county? Such questions can lead to new directions in the quest.

Practical work

During the week you spend on this lesson, review all the information you have gathered about mysterious phenomena in the area you are studying, paying special attention to dates and places. See if you can identify specific flaps or windows from the data.

Question for reflection

Why do you think unexplained phenomena tend to cluster in space and time, instead of being more evenly distributed?

LESSON 48

Between two worlds

Seed thought

No one can claim to know all the answers. But we are finally learning to ask the right questions.
—John Keel, *Strange Creatures from Time and Space*

Orientation

1. One of the basic concepts of occult philosophy, as discussed in the second lesson of this book, is the recognition that the world of matter and energy we experience with our five ordinary senses is only a part, and a small part at that, of the whole cosmos that human beings inhabit. Books of occult teaching very often divide the cosmos into various planes, regions, or states of being, each of which influences human life and consciousness in its own way. For the purposes of this book, however, it is enough to recognize two worlds, which we can call simply the Seen and the Unseen.
2. The sites, stories, and phenomena you have researched over the past year can all be understood as points of contact between these two worlds. Sites, whether they are places of ancient sanctity or simply

locations where strange things have happened or strange stories are set, represent points of contact between the Unseen and the physical landscape. In an old but still useful way of speaking, these are places where the veil between the worlds is thin, and what is normally invisible to us can occasionally be glimpsed.
3. Stories represent points of contact between the Unseen and the world of human culture—more specifically, the folk culture of those who live in a particular region. This is especially true of those stories that are rich in archetypal material. Here, too, the veil between the worlds is thin, but in a different sense. Folk memories of past phenomena combine with the influence of the human mind's deep places to make stories a mirror in which the movements of the Unseen can very often be glimpsed, and sometimes even understood.
4. Phenomena, finally, represent points of contact between the Unseen and the realm of immediate human experience. These are the most obvious and dramatic thin places in the veil between the worlds. When something that theoretically can't or doesn't exist shows itself to startled human witnesses, the Unseen briefly becomes part of the Seen, and demonstrates in a definitive way the frail nature of our concepts of reality.
5. Sites, stories, and phenomena each tell us something about the nature of the Unseen as it expresses itself in a particular region of the earth's surface. As individual data points, they often communicate little beyond a general sense of the strangeness of the cosmos. Put them together a piece at a time and they trace out an invisible landscape that parallels the visible landscape exactly. The narrative landscape discussed in an earlier lesson is a human effort to express part of that vaster invisible terrain.
6. Your work over the year just past has been an exploration of that invisible landscape, using sites, stories, and phenomena as points of access to the Unseen. During that process you have had the opportunity to catch glimpses of the invisible landscape and to gain some sense of how it influences human life in general, and if you followed the advice in the introduction, of how it shapes your life in particular. A sense of the magical dimensions of place is an important skill for the practicing occultist, and can be used to guide study and practice.
7. In a very real sense, a knowledge of the magical dimensions of place fills the same role as a knowledge of the unseen dimensions of time, as expressed in occult arts such as astrology and numerology.

The great difference between these two kinds of knowledge is simply that the hidden side of time is tolerably well understood by students of occultism, while the hidden side of place is not. Your work during the past year, and the work of earth mysteries researchers generally, is part of a major project of rediscovery: the restoration of the old occult knowledge of the powers of place. If you choose, you can take the skills you have learned during this year and apply them to that project more generally. The choice, however, is up to you.

Practical work

During the week you spend on this lesson, review all that you have learned and studied about the earth mysteries of the area you've researched over the past year. See to what extent you can synthesize the results of your research. Notice the places where sites, stories, and phenomena overlap, and the places where they apparently have nothing to do with one another. Consider writing a short essay summarizing the presence of the Unseen in the part of the earth's surface you have studied.

Question for reflection

What have you learned from the year you have spent studying earth mysteries?

FOUR SAMPLE EXPLORATIONS

Preliminary note

As mentioned earlier, it is not enough to read about other people's adventures with the sites, stories, and phenomena that make up the field of earth mysteries. Part of the process of working through this book will consist of your own investigations into the earth mysteries of the region in which you live. You should plan on carrying out at least four such investigations during the year you spend on this book, and spend a week meditating on the results of each of these investigations.

Since each such investigation will be different, it is impossible to give strict rules for how to conduct them. Instead, I have included four examples of my own earth mysteries investigations here.

These are among other things examples of what can be done in a small and not especially legend-packed area. Rhode Island, where I live, is far and away the smallest state in the Union.* Partly because of its small size, it is less richly supplied with sites, stories, and phenomena than most other parts of the country. Even so, I had to choose among well over a dozen sites, stories, and phenomena. The ones I picked were those that tied most closely into my interests, on the one hand, and turned out to have a reasonable amount of information available, on the other. Feel free to use similar criteria to select the earth mysteries you investigate.

---

*British readers may find it helpful to know that Rhode Island is a little larger than Oxfordshire.

SAMPLE EXPLORATION 1

The legend of William Blackstone

Most histories of Rhode Island start by talking about the native peoples of the area, the Narragansett and Wampanoag nations, and leap from there immediately to the colorful religious eccentric Roger Williams, who founded the Rhode Island colony. Lost in the space between is the remarkable figure of Rev. William Blackstone (also spelled Blaxton), the first European settler in what became Rhode Island, who became the focus of curious legends during his lifetime and thereafter.

Evidence

Blackstone was born in Lincolnshire in 1598, attended Emmanuel College, Cambridge from 1614 to 1621, and was ordained a priest in the Church of England. In 1623 he joined an expedition to the New World, serving as chaplain, but when the other members of the expedition fled back to England in 1625, Blackstone stayed behind. On the site where the city of Boston would later rise, he built a house for himself with his own hands, and lived there in comfortable solitude until 1630, when the Puritans arrived and settled down near him.

By 1635 his disagreements with the dour and dogmatic Puritans had become serious enough that he sold his land to the newly founded city of Boston and left. (The land became Boston Common, a famous public park in downtown Boston.) Some thirty-five miles south of the colony, in what was then dense forest, he built a new house for himself atop a low hill, which he called Study Hill, and settled down again to a solitary life. He raised cattle, tended a garden, studied his books, and bred the first apple variety native to the New World, the Yellow Sweeting. His library, which had its own building on Study Hill, was for many years the largest collection of books in the American colonies.

When other white settlers began to find their way to Rhode Island, Blackstone became a legendary figure among them. He was said to ride through the woods on the back of a placid white bull, reading one of his books as the animal strolled along, carrying a sack of apples to hand out to native and settler children alike. In old age he married a young widow, Sarah Fisher Stevenson, and had a son with her. He died in 1675, just before the fragile peace between the settlers and the native peoples finally shattered and King Philip's War broke out. His house and library were burnt to the ground in the fighting.

Discussion

William Blackstone was unquestionably a historical person. His role in local legend and folklore, however, shows that he became a magnet for archetypal imagery. Outside of a rodeo, bulls are not riding animals—they are far too temperamental—but the image of the wise man riding a bull can be found in various mystical traditions as an emblem of the power of consciousness over the animal passions. Zen Buddhism and Taoism have both made use of this imagery; in traditional China and Japan, no one would have had the least problem making sense of Blackstone's life.

The pairing of man and bull has another resonance in the realm of creation myth. Far back in time, Indo-European mythologies imagined the first created beings to be a man and a cow or bull: Norse mythology features the original giant Ymir and the primal cow Audhumla, for example, while the myths of ancient Persia assign the same role to the first man Gayomart and the first bull Gaw-i-Ewdad. Thus it is interesting, to use no stronger term, that here in Rhode Island a man and a bull show up at the beginning of European settlement, as a secular echo of these mythic patterns.

THE LEGEND OF WILLIAM BLACKSTONE   205

It is also interesting to note that according to unpublished notes of Ross Nichols, one of the most influential Druid teachers of the last century, one of the most ancient names of Britain was "the Land of the White Bull." Rhode Island is not Britain but, as will be discussed in the second of these explorations, there is a remarkable geological connection between this part of New England, on the one hand, and Wales and southern England on the other. Did the Land of the White Bull once reach across the ocean? Or did it somehow move west in the course of the passing ages?

Another archetype with more of a presence in the American imagination shows itself in the connection between Blackstone and the Yellow Sweeting apple. The image of the lone white man traveling through the wilderness, in perfect harmony with his surroundings, handing out apples to Native Americans and colonists alike, found its classic expression in the life of John Chapman, the "Johnny Appleseed" of American legend—another historical figure who became a magnet for archetypal forces. Blackstone was another manifestation of the same mythic image.

Behind them both stands the far more ancient figure of Myrddin Wyllt, the "wild Merlin" of Welsh and Breton legend. Before he was cleaned up and turned into King Arthur's pet wizard, Merlin was a stranger and more uncanny personage, a shamanic figure who dwelt in the wilderness with a wolf for companion and, yes, apple trees for sustenance. One of the archaic Welsh poems traditionally credited to Myrddin Wyllt is titled *Yr Afallenau* ("The Apple Trees"); in translation, each of its stanzas begins with the words "Sweet apple tree."

Finally, Blackstone shares with Merlin and many other figures of myth and legend an odd postmortem destiny: nobody knows where his remains are located. In 1888, Study Hill fell victim to the ongoing expansion of Rhode Island's then-booming industrial economy, and the entire hill was leveled to the ground to make room for a new factory. A twelve-foot granite obelisk commemorating him was placed on the factory grounds. Blackstone's remains were disinterred before the demolition of the hill, but no record indicates whether they were placed beneath the monument when it went up. In 1943, when the factory had become a rundown naval repair depot, the monument was moved to a nearby location on Broad Street, and in 1996 it was moved again to its present site. Nobody seems to know whether the remains accompanied the monument in the first move, and there is no evidence that anyone even looked for them when it came time for the second. As befits a mythic being, he has no grave.

Investigation

As just noted, Study Hill no longer exists. Its location is now the village of Lonsdale in Lincoln, Rhode Island, a greener-than-average postindustrial New England landscape of old brick factory buildings put to new uses, and equally old wood frame houses serving their original function. The exact location of the hill no longer seems to be known.

The present Blackstone Memorial Park is located half a mile northeast at the intersection of Broad Street and Blackstone Street, just north of Valley Falls, Rhode Island. It is a small but pleasant space with young trees sheltering a little circular plaza of brick and the old battered base of the original Blackstone monument—the twelve-foot obelisk is among the other things that got lost in the course of the various relocations. In good weather, it's a pleasant place to sit and meditate; if you wear ordinary clothes and do nothing to draw attention to yourself, passersby will assume that you're just enjoying a little fresh air.

On the inner planes, by contrast, Study Hill still exists and can be visited in scrying and other visionary states. If my experience is anything to go by, the easiest way there is to start by building up clearly in your mind's eye an image of what that part of Rhode Island looked like when William Blackstone first lived there. Imagine a thick forest of oak, elm, chestnut, and pine, with rays of sunlight slanting down through gaps in the leaf cover. Make the image as tangible as possible, so that you feel the ground beneath your feet and the breeze on your skin, hear the rustling of the leaves, smell the scents of soil and tree bark. Since Blackstone spent most of his life dwelling in the wilderness, it's essential to attune to the forest he knew.

The first time I did this, I sat on a fallen log and simply waited. Some time passed before I heard the slow beat of hooves on the forest floor. That got louder, and then a large white bull came into sight, walking calmly through the woods. Perched on its back without benefit of saddle was a middle-aged man in plain brown clothing of seventeenth-century cut, a book open in his hand, paying no attention to the path the bull took. I got to my feet as the bull approached. The man glanced up, unsurprised, and touched the bull with one hand. It stopped, and I had a brief conversation with the Reverend William Blackstone, or rather with his astral image.

Most of that conversation is irrelevant to the subject of this book and will not be repeated here. One detail worth passing on is that, in this vision, Blackstone's image said that he studied mystical and occult books before he left for America. If this is correct, he was part of a significant American tradition: quite a few of the legendary forest-dwelling hermits of the colonial and federal periods of United States history, including John "Johnny Appleseed" Chapman himself, were influenced by occult teachings and played a role in transmitting those teachings to the New World. I have not yet been able to verify this detail of the vision in historical records, but it may offer useful angles for further research.

Getting there

By car: Take I-95 north from Providence to Exit 40. From there, take RI-122 north for three miles, then turn right on Ann & Hope Way; turn left after a third of a mile onto Broad Street, and look for the park on the right, just past the Blackstone River Theater building.

By bus: From Kennedy Plaza Transit Center in Providence, take the R circulator bus north to the Pawtucket-Central Falls Transit Center, and take the 71 north from there to the intersection of Broad Street and Ann & Hope Way. Walk north along Broad Street, past the Blackstone River Theater building; the park is on the right.

From the park, Lonsdale is an easy half-mile walk. Half a block south on Broad Street brings you to Ann & Hope Way; turn right and follow Ann & Hope Way west for a quarter mile, crossing the Blackstone River, and then turn left onto Mendon Road. Another quarter mile or so and you're in the middle of Lonsdale, as close to Study Hill as any material means of transport can get you in the present age.

Sources

Blackstone 1974, Lind 1993, Rhode's Gallery 2018.

SAMPLE EXPLORATION 2

The Glocester dragon

Mysterious nonhuman creatures tend to be even more closely tied to place than other strange phenomena. While individual ghosts are strictly placebound, ghosts of the same basic types are seen all over the world, so are aerial lights of every kind, and Charles Fort recorded fishes and frogs falling from the sky in many different places. Yet the Jersey Devil, Mothman, and most other monstrous beings are far less likely to be sighted away from their usual grounds.

The classic European dragon, winged, scaled, guarding treasure, and breathing fire from its fanged muzzle, is one of these highly localized creatures. While dragons of various kinds are found all over the world, only the most inattentive observer would mistake a European dragon for the sinuous, wingless dragon of China and Japan or the feathered serpent of Mexico and central America. This makes it all the more remarkable that Rhode Island can boast one of the very few sightings outside Europe of the kind of dragon that Beowulf and Sigurd fought.

Evidence

The dragon in question was encountered near the small town of Glocester,* Rhode Island in 1839, and again in 1896. The 1839 sighting is particularly famous because the man who reported it, Albert Hicks, was one of the last people to be hanged for piracy in the United States. Before the hangman's rope sent him on to his next incarnation on July 13, 1860, he talked at length to reporters, and one of the stories he told—reprinted many years later in a story in the *Evening Hour*, a Connecticut newspaper—included a hair-raising encounter with one of the world's classic monsters.

In 1839 Hicks was a boy in Foster, Rhode Island, with his head full of dreams of pirate treasure. Plenty of people had such dreams, because the golden age of piracy had ended just a century before, and the colonies that became the United States had been one vast pirate haven in the century or so before independence. The idea that some of those pirates had left buried treasure behind was on many minds in Hicks's time.

Hicks and three of his cronies, John Jepp, Ben Cobb, and Ben Saunders, were among those. They became convinced that the notorious Captain Kidd had hidden some of his treasure on a farm in the nearby town of Glocester. The four boys got shovels and lanterns, and one dark and moonless night headed over to the farm to try to find the treasure. What they found was something else again. The account from the newspaper story runs as follows:

"It was a large animal, with staring eyes as big as pewter bowls. The eyes looked like balls of fire. When it breathed as it went by, flames came out of its mouth and nostrils, scorching the brush in its path. It was as big as a cow with dark wings on each side like a bat's. It had spiral horns like a ram's, as big around as a stovepipe. Its feet were formed like a duck's and measured a foot and a half across. The body was covered with scales as big as clamshells, which made a rattling noise as the beast moved along. The scales flapped up and down. The thing had lights on its sides like those shining through a tin lantern. Before I saw it I felt its presence and I smelled something that was like burnt wool as it went by. I had a feeling of suffocation when it came near me. The monster seemed to come out of nowhere and to go away in the same manner."

---

*For some reason this has always been spelled without the usual U after the O. Rhode Island is like that; it's supposed to be named after the Greek island of Rhodes, but nobody has ever used the final S.

Hicks and his friends understandably took to their heels and kept running until they got safely back to Foster. Fifty-seven years passed before the dragon stirred again.

This time the witness was an ordinary resident of Glocester, Neil Hopkins, who reported a similar experience one cold January night when he was on his way home from work in Putnam, just across the border in Connecticut. Something he thought was as large as an elephant chased him for a short distance and then vanished into the woods. The newspaper story quoted Hopkins's breathless words: "It seemed to be all a-fire; it had a hot breath. There was a metallic sound, like the clanking of steel against steel. The beast didn't seem to be strong in the wind, for it chased me only a short distance, and then plunged off into the woods. I could hear the dead branches and twigs crackling under the heavy tramp."

This was the last reported encounter with Glocester's dragon. According to the same newspaper story, however, "there are many people in Glocester who believe that the beast still haunts the forest not far from the Providence turnpike." Since Hicks didn't give the location of the farm in Glocester, it is possible that he and his cronies met the dragon in this same area: in the northwest part of Glocester, just south of the main road from Providence through Glocester to Putnam, Connecticut, which is now US Highway 44.

One other oddity surrounds this remarkable creature: its name in folklore. For some reason most media accounts of it, dating back to the 1890s, call it the Glocester Ghoul. A ghoul, for the benefit of those readers who aren't familiar with monster lore, is a humanlike creature in Arabic tradition who haunts graveyards and dines on the dead, with the occasional living person added to the menu from time to time. I know of no description of ghouls that gives them scales, ram's horns, batlike wings, or fiery breath. Most likely the name was coined by some nineteenth-century journalist who thought it sounded good and didn't care about the details.

Discussion

Dragons of one kind or another appear in legend all over the world, and now and then people report seeing one. What exactly is seen, however, varies by region. The standard European dragon, of the kind immortalized in the pages of *Beowulf* and *The Hobbit*, is apparently not found outside of Europe. Dragon sightings in eastern Asia are inevitably of

Asian dragons, which are long, wingless, antlered, and far less malevolent than their European equivalents. Similarly, most American dragon sightings correspond closely to Native American traditions about serpentlike creatures, which diverge considerably among themselves but have little in common with the sort of dragon Sigurd the Volsung slew. The dragon of Glocester is thus an anomaly even among anomalies.

An odd detail of geology, however, may offer a perspective on this puzzle. Most of today's continents include fragments of far more ancient land masses that were scooped up via the process of continental drift. The state of Rhode Island is part of one of these. Originally an island chain the size of Japan, the land mass that today's geologists call Avalonia first rose from archaic seas while multicellular life forms were beginning to evolve on earth. Continental drift sent it skidding across the planet, moving about the speed that fingernails grow, until finally it was caught between two other continents, the ancestors of today's Europe and North America. When those separated again, ancient Avalonia was divided between them.

That is why a strip of land along the east coast of North America from Rhode Island north to Newfoundland is geologically identical to another strip of land extending from the southern edge of Ireland east to Wales, southern England, Belgium, the Netherlands, and the northern edges of Germany and Poland. Those are the places where the fragments of ancient Avalonia ended up. The fragments east of the Atlantic are the homelands of the classic European dragon. If dragons and dragon legends are at least partly shaped by the subtle influences of the land, it makes sense that a fragment of Avalonia west of the Atlantic would host a dragon of similar type.

There is of course another possibility. In its two known appearances, the Glocester dragon behaved in the same very curious way: it suddenly appeared, ran in a straight line for a short distance, and then vanished. In both cases it made metallic clanking sounds, and seemed to have fire within it. If someone manufactured a fake dragon using nineteenth-century technology, the accounts of Hicks and Hopkins would be plausible descriptions of such a device. Its pattern of movement suggests that it might have run on rails, or on a steel cable or strong wire stretched between stout trees.

This suggestion raises any number of questions, however. Most hoaxers like to show off their skill at frequent intervals—more frequent, certainly, than the fifty-seven-year gap between the dragon's appearances. If the dragon was not simply an elaborate practical joke, though, what was its purpose? Why did its owner choose to show it to four boys out on a lark, an ordinary citizen on his way home from work, and nobody else? I have not been able to find answers to these questions. The nature of the Glocester dragon therefore remains a mystery.

Investigation

Western Rhode Island is not the kind of place that makes life easy for the investigator of earth mysteries. You don't count as local, or so the saying has it, unless all of your grandparents were born there. The people of Glocester are gracious to guests but they are fine examples of the rural New England population, and stubborn silence is one of the region's hallmarks. If backwoods New Englanders don't want to talk about something, you really are better off having a conversation with a brick wall.

Certainly no one I spoke to on the subject of the Glocester dragon had anything relevant to say about it. As an outsider with a West Coast accent, of course, I had two strikes against me, so this came as no surprise. The documentary sources I was able to find simply repeated the newspaper account quoted above, sometimes accurately, sometimes with insertions or deletions for which no reason was given. As for occult methods of investigation, I attempted several of these and got nothing more than various reflections of the modern collective imagination. If the secret of the Glocester dragon can still be found, someone else will have to find it.

Getting there

By car: US 44 runs straight out from just north of downtown Providence. Once you're past the little village of Chepachet, you're in Glocester dragon territory.

By bus: Rhode Island's otherwise fine public transit system doesn't extend far into the forests of the western part of the state. If you use public transportation, as I do, your best bet is to take the 58 bus from Kennedy Plaza Transit Center in Providence to Smithfield Crossing and then plan on a ten mile hike along the shoulders of US 44 to the area once haunted by the dragon. If you want to make a weekend of it, the White Rock Motel a little over a mile east of Chepachet on US 44 is convenient and pleasant.

Sources

Anonymous 1896; Arnold 2010; Girard 2017; Ocker 2022.

SAMPLE EXPLORATION 3

The Newport Tower enigma

Rhode Island has a fair collection of archaic stone ruins, some of which were certainly put there by the local Native Americans, while others have no known origin. Then there is the Newport Tower, a stone tower which stands today in the middle of a park just above downtown Newport, Rhode Island. After at least four centuries of ordinary weathering and the demolition of its upper story by gunpowder, it still stands some twenty-eight feet tall. Its design—a round tower supported on eight sturdy pillars separated by open archways—and its stonework suggest a European origin. The great question that has sparked controversy over the tower is whether it was built after the official settlement of the region, or before.

The evidence

The tower itself sits in the middle of Touro Park, a pleasant green space on a hill overlooking downtown Newport; before the town spread around it, the location had a fine view of Newport harbor and the mouth of Narragansett Bay. The tower itself, some twenty-four feet across at its base, is built of local stones solidly mortared together, and probably once had a layer of plaster covering the stones inside and out, though weathering removed all but a few traces of this centuries ago. Though it is open to the sky today, stone piers and sockets inside show that it once had wooden floors resting on large timber beams, and testimony from early days indicates that it also once had a roof. Above the pillars and arches, the wall is pierced by small windows at odd intervals. There are also niches built into the walls, and a stone fireplace with two flues designed to vent smoke outside.

Recent research has shown that the windows are much less random than they look. They are aligned on various positions of the sun and moon, allowing the spring and autumn equinoxes and the summer and winter solstices to be measured exactly, and also track several lunar cycles. Some researchers have referred to the tower as "Rhode Island's Stonehenge," and the Knights Templar branch of the Freemasons in Rhode Island hold an annual ceremony around the tower each year on the winter solstice.

Documentary evidence concerning the tower's early days is difficult to come by, for the simple reason that many of Newport's town records did not survive the Revolutionary War. The British held Newport from 1776 to 1779, they took the town records with them when they finally evacuated their force by sea, and the ship carrying the records went to the bottom during the voyage. Some of them were recovered from the wreck and made legible again, but much was lost. The scraps of data that remain, however, suggest that there may well have been a tower on Aquidneck Island before the founding of the town of Newport.

A petition to the English crown for a grant of lands on Long Island and the nearby mainland by Sir Edmund Plowden in 1632, for example, references a "round stone towre." The petition is vague enough in its geography that it's impossible to tell whether the "towre" is supposed to be on Long Island or the mainland, but there is no evidence for a stone tower anywhere on Long Island, and there is only one such tower that might have existed on the mainland at that date—the Newport Tower.

Similarly, a 1635 map of the region by William Wood shows a town named "Old Plymouth" on the eastern shores of Narragansett Bay, not far from the current location of Newport—and marks the location of Old Plymouth by a little sketch of a stone tower. (The Plymouth that every American schoolchild learns about, the one on the Massachusetts coast, is called "New Plymouth" on Wood's map.) No other surviving record mentions an earlier Plymouth Colony in the region, and Newport and the land around it was not settled by English colonists until 1639, when a band of dissident Pilgrims from Massachusetts Bay moved there.

The next reference to the tower in surviving documents dates from 1677. In that year a local dignitary named Benedict Arnold—the grandfather of the famous Revolutionary War traitor—drew up a will mentioning his "stone bilt wind miln." From this point on the chain of possession is fairly clear, and the "wind miln" appears to have been the Newport Tower. Plenty of contemporary evidence shows that the tower was in fact used as the base of a windmill in Arnold's time and for some decades thereafter.

Most mainstream historians insist on this basis that the tower must have been built by Arnold, but of course this hardly follows. Colonial New Englanders were adept at repurposing old structures for new uses; the Newport Tower itself was later repurposed as a military watchtower, the British army during the Revolutionary War used it as a gunpowder magazine (and accidentally blew off the tower's upper story in the process), and in between these uses it was put to work as a haymow—that is, a place where hay could be stacked after cutting to dry. It is certainly possible that Arnold built it, but just as possible that he took an existing tower and reused it by putting a windmill on top of it.

Archeological excavations around the tower in 1948 found English coins dating between 1696 and 1702, bits of millstone, loose plaster fragments, and a great many animal bones. The soil around the tower was much disturbed by digging and other human activities before Touro Park was created, however, and it is by no means certain that everything found in the dig dated from the foundation of the tower.

One final source of equivocal data comes from radiocarbon dating. The mortar used to build the tower contains small amounts of organic material, and this can be dated to within half a century or so by the standard carbon-14 method. Samples of the mortar were taken in 1993 and tested, and returned a date somewhere between 1635 and 1698. It cannot be determined, however, whether this was the original mortar used to build the tower, or later mortar used for repointing (refilling gaps between stones with fresh mortar), or a mixture of the two.

Discussion

There are plenty of theories about the origin of the Newport Tower. The one accepted by most mainstream historians, as noted above, is the claim that the tower was built by Benedict Arnold sometime before 1677 as a windmill. The arguments supporting this theory are curiously circular: defenders of the theory insist that the oldest reliable record of the tower is Arnold's 1677 will, but this is only true once they dismiss all earlier references to the tower as unreliable. It certainly seems to be the case that the tower was used as a windmill, but as noted above, this does not mean that it was built as one. There were, as it happens, no other stone-built tower windmills anywhere in colonial America; windmills were normally made of wood in that era.

Leave behind the officially approved wipe and the theories come thick and fast. The oldest is the claim that the tower was built by Norse explorers. This was first proposed in 1839 by Thomas Webb, then secretary of the Rhode Island Historical Association, and has been supported by many alternative historians since that time. Certainly the Norse reached the New World and explored several areas in what are now the Maritime Provinces of Canada; records of their visits have been preserved in Icelandic sagas, and several archeological sites have revealed physical signs of their presence.

Another theory has been floated by Gavin Menzies, who has written several books claiming that a Chinese fleet circumnavigated the globe in the early fifteenth century and left various mysterious sites in coastal spots around the world. Menzies is probably correct that Chinese maritime exploration at this time covered more territory than conventional historians like to admit, but he has taken his claims considerably further than the evidence will permit; I would not be especially surprised to hear him insist that fifteenth-century Chinese fleets landed on the moon. The Newport Tower is built in a European architectural style, not in any style practiced by the Chinese. Barring significant new evidence, his claim should probably be set aside as extremely improbable.

Still another theory, with a good deal more plausibility, suggests that the tower was built by Knights Templar who escaped from the destruction of their order by the King of France in 1314. A mystery has long surrounded the Templar fleet based in the French port of La Rochelle; the Templar order kept ships there to transport soldiers and goods from their English and Scottish possessions to Europe and the Holy Land. When the Templars were rounded up by Henri IV's officers, however, the fleet seems to have disappeared. Its destination remains unknown to this day.

Several alternative historians in recent years have explored the possibility that the Templars pursued a program of maritime exploration westward, along the same lines that the Portuguese, Spanish, and British did in the next century. The Azores and the Caribbean islands have been discussed as the most likely endpoints of this project, but a few researchers have made arguments for a Templar presence further north along the American coast. The Newport Tower with its eight pillars is a plausible Templar construction, as the Templars made a specialty of stone construction and many Templar churches have a similar circular design.

A third theory credits the tower to Portuguese mariners at the beginning of the sixteenth century, a few years after Columbus's famous voyage. The Portuguese began a well-documented program of oceanic exploration early in the fifteenth century, under the leadership of the famous Prince Henry the Navigator. Their ships were perfectly capable of making the Atlantic crossing—Portuguese mariners were the first Europeans to voyage around Africa to India, a considerably longer voyage—and Portuguese fishermen were catching codfish off Newfoundland by the 1470s. Evidence from old Portuguese maps and a handful of physical artifacts make a strong case that Portuguese ships had explored the southern coast of New England before 1510. There are structures in Portugal very similar to the Newport Tower, and it has been proposed by several scholars that a Portuguese expedition in 1501–1502 might have built the tower.

There are fascinating points of contact between this theory and the Templar theory. Portugal was one of only two countries in Europe that refused to suppress the Templar order when the pope ordered it to be disbanded. (The other was Scotland.) Portugal's King Denis arranged for all the Templars in Portugal, along with all their assets and properties, to be transferred into a newly founded order, the Order of Christ, which remains in existence to this day. The Order of Christ proceeded to play a central role in the Portuguese voyages of exploration; unsurprisingly, Prince Henry the Navigator was the Order's Grand Master for many years. The possibility that information about the Atlantic acquired by the Templars in the Middle East might have been preserved by the Knights of Christ, and played a significant role in launching the Age of Discovery, deserves more attention than it has yet received.

Another intriguing theory has been proposed by researcher Jim Egan, who runs a small private museum close to the tower. Using documentary sources ranging from English court records to the reports of Spanish spies, Egan has shown that a nearly forgotten English expedition of 1582 headed by Anthony Brigham set out to establish an English colony on Narragansett Bay. The project was under the patronage of

Sir Humphrey Gilbert, but it was largely planned by Queen Elizabeth's court wizard John Dee.

The 1582 voyage was a preliminary venture, and was to be followed the next year by a larger expedition to make the settlement permanent. Unfortunately, the 1583 expedition under Humphrey Gilbert was a total failure. One ship had to turn back a day out of port because of illness, a second was wrecked on a sandbar, a third had to be sent back to England with more sick men, and when Gilbert finally sailed for home without ever reaching Narragansett Bay, his ship went down with all hands in a hurricane, leaving only one ship to limp back home. The project Gilbert and Dee had drafted was abandoned thereafter, and decades passed before the first successful English colony was founded at Jamestown.

The Newport Tower, Egan proposes, was built by Anthony Brigham and his men in 1582–1583, using a design drawn up by John Dee. It was intended to be the central structure of an English colonial town. Dee, who was among other things an expert in optics and astronomy, designed the tower windows so that they could be used by the colonists to track the seasons and provide such Elizabethan necessities as an accurate date for Easter each year. The failure of the project left the tower as the only legacy of England's first attempt to colonize the New World.

Which of these theories is correct? So far, nobody knows. The Newport Tower remains, as it was first called more than a century ago, "the most enigmatic and puzzling building in the United States of America."*

The investigation

The Newport Tower has been the subject of countless inquiries and investigations spanning nearly two centuries. These days it is visited by thousands of tourists every year, and has a wrought iron fence around it to keep it safe from vandalism. My visit there on the physical plane did not turn up any new evidence—nor, to be fair, did I expect it to do so. My investigation into the tower, on the historical side, mostly consisted of reading the voluminous literature on the subject, and this gave me a good sense of the many controversies surrounding the Newport Tower but brought no firm conclusions—though I did find some of the theories considerably more plausible than others.

On the occult side of the investigation, I attempted to use psychometry to catch some glimpse of the tower's past. The object I used was

---

*Brigham 1948, p. 32.

a small fragment of stone found in the park, which appeared to be made of the same stone as the tower itself. When I psychometrized the stone, I saw a vivid image of a man in coarse brown woolen clothing: a loose coat or smock and a pair of trousers going below the knees. He had reddish-brown hair and a roughly cut short beard of the same color. I could not see his surroundings clearly, but he was looking off into the distance, and then turned and spoke to someone who was not visible to me.

I could not hear the words but I could sense the meaning. He and others had been keeping watch for ships for a long time—more than a year, possibly more than a few years. No ships had appeared, and he was telling the other person that the ships would not come and that they had no choice but to go live with the local Native American people. He then turned away. I had the sense that he had a wife and family somewhere else that he knew he would never see again, and that he planned on marrying a Native American woman and making the best life he could in the New World.

The vision ended at that point and I was not able to obtain any other images from the stone. Whether or not it was an actual glimpse into the history of the Newport Tower will have to be left to other investigators to determine.

Getting there

By car: From Providence, take I-195 a little over sixteen miles east across the state line to Exit 14A, and from there continue south on state route 24—it has the same number in Massachusetts and Rhode Island. Merge onto West Main Road and keep going. After seven miles West Main turns into Broadway, and then the directions get complex: turn left onto Gibbs Avenue, then right onto Kay Street, then left onto Bellevue Avenue, which goes right past the park.

By bus: Routes 14 and 60 run from Kennedy Plaza Transit Center in Providence to downtown Newport, and from the final stop it's an easy walk to the tower: south along America's Cup Avenue to Mill Street for the first, south along Farewell Street, Touro Street, and Spring Street to Mill Street for the second. If you get lost, ask the locals to point you toward Mill Street, which also goes right past the park.

Sources

Brigham 1948, Da Silva 1971, Egan 2011.

SAMPLE EXPLORATION 4

The lost city of Norumbega

The Newport Tower is a site that cannot be identified with any known legend. The city of Norumbega, by contrast, is a legend that cannot be identified with any known site. From the time of the first European voyages to North America until the beginning of large-scale British settlement of the Atlantic seaboard, European maps included references to a Native American city called Norumbega, which was supposedly located somewhere on what is now the coast of New England. Several early European explorers claimed to have visited Norumbega and traded with its inhabitants, and brought back detailed, colorful descriptions of the city and its people. No trace of such a city has been found by archeologists, however. It remains one of the great enigmas of the northern Atlantic states.

The evidence

The name "Norumbega" is apparently a garbled version of a word in one of the Algonquian languages of Native New England, and has been translated as "place of still waters." The first known European visitor to the city was Giovanni da Verrazano, an Italian captain working for the Spanish government, who claimed to have landed there in 1524. His brother Girolamo published a map of the New World in 1529 which shows the city of "Oranbega" located somewhere vaguely northeast of Virginia.

In 1543 a French mariner, Jean Alfonse, described the country and city of Norumbega in some detail. He claimed that it was on a river estuary, some fifteen leagues (around forty-five miles) from the sea; the estuary was around forty leagues (120 miles) wide and full of many islands. Its people, who were tall and handsome, worshipped the sun, spoke a language that sounded a little like Latin, and had become rich through the fur trade.

The most talkative witness of Norumbega in its prime was an English sailor named David Ingram. In 1568, he was stranded on what is now the coast of Texas after the British privateer fleet in which he served was mauled in a naval battle by the Spanish. He and some fifty other sailors set out to walk to what is now New England, where British and French fishing vessels routinely landed at that time. Most of them died or gave up the journey and settled among the native peoples of the continent, but Ingram and two others reached what is now eastern Canada, where they were rescued by a French ship.

We don't have Ingram's own account of his journey. He was apparently illiterate, and his words were taken down by Queen Elizabeth's spymaster and spin doctor Sir Francis Walsingham and published in 1583 as *A True Discourse of the Adventures and Travailes of David Ingram*. No copy of this book is known to survive, but some parts of it were included in Richard Hakluyt's classic 1589 account *The Principall Navigations, Voiages and Discoveries of the English Nation*. The version in Hakluyt combines detailed and fairly accurate accounts of the Native American nations of the Mississippi valley and the eastern seaboard with improbable details—for example, he claimed to have encountered elephants and horses, and reported that some coastal cities were visited now and then by merchant ships from China.

Whether these details were inserted by Walsingham or Hakluyt to support the then-popular claim of a Northwest Passage connecting North America to East Asia is anyone's guess, but the possibility cannot be dismissed out of hand. According to the account as we have it, though, Ingram encountered thriving towns and cities all through Native North America. The most impressive of the cities was Norumbega, which was located on the Atlantic coast somewhere well south of what is now the

St. Lawrence seaway. According to the account, the city of Norumbega was half a mile long, and its streets were wider than the narrow winding thoroughfares of Elizabethan London.

Two British explorers, John Walker and Stephen Bellinger, claimed that they reached Norumbega in 1580 and 1583 respectively and traded with its inhabitants. Maps of the region all through the late sixteenth and early seventeenth centuries accordingly included the city of Norumbega along with other landmarks along the Atlantic seaboard, such as "Chesipeoc Bay" and a cape named "Hatorask." Some such maps also include a "Fort Norumbega" located somewhere close to the mouth of the estuary that led to the city.

When the voyage of the *Mayflower* in 1620 inaugurated the first great wave of British settlement of New England, however, Norumbega was nowhere to be found. Historians and mapmakers in later years accordingly dismissed Norumbega as a fable. By and large, they still do so today.

The second half of the nineteenth century saw the story of Norumbega revived by students of alternative history interested in Norse voyages to America before the time of Columbus. Making use of dubious etymology, they translated the name to mean "city of the Norse" and claimed to locate it in various corners of northern New England from Bangor, Maine south to the Boston area. While there is ample evidence for Norse landings and settlements in some parts of far eastern Canada, no evidence for a Norse city corresponding to Norumbega was ever successfully located.

The context

Until relatively recently it was standard to dismiss David Ingram's account of a Native America full of thriving urban centers as so much nonsense. Archeological research during the last half century or so, however, has shown that he was simply reporting what he saw. The so-called Mound Builder cultures of Native North America were a historical reality in Ingram's time, with powerful, populous cities all through the Mississippi River basin. He was among the few European people to see them in their prime, however, for smallpox and other Old World diseases swept through the continent repeatedly during the seventeenth century, reducing the native population to 5% or less of its pre-contact levels.

In less than 100 years, sheer demographic collapse reduced thriving urban agricultural societies all over North and South America to scattered bands of shell-shocked survivors, who then had to cope with the rising tide of mass immigration from Europe. Urban centers, with their densely packed populations, have always been hit more heavily by epidemic diseases than more widely dispersed rural populations. Under the circumstances, it's far from impossible that a large urban center in Native New England could have vanished completely between 1583 and 1620, especially if it was built of wood, the standard building material among the eastern tribes.

One detail passed on by Jean Alfonse is especially important in thinking about pre-collapse Norumbega. He noted that the wealth of the city came from the fur trade. As soon as European ships began crossing the Atlantic, furs became one of the most profitable cargoes they carried back to Europe. This trade may well have begun even before Columbus's first voyage in 1492, as English and Portuguese ships were already crossing to Newfoundland by then and bringing back cargoes of codfish from the Grand Banks; furs purchased from local tribes would have been a welcome source of profit for any such voyage.

It is therefore at least worth exploring the possibility that Norumbega was a center of the fur trade, where pelts gathered by Native American tribes all through New England were sold to eager European ship captains. History shows that in any situation where great wealth suddenly flows through an area, boomtowns arise quickly and can become very rich. When the wealth disappears—when, for example, the fur-bearing animals in a region are trapped out and the fur trade shifts to another, less depleted region, or when warfare or epidemic disease disrupts trade routes—boomtowns vanish just as quickly.

The greatest uncertainty about Norumbega is its location. The maps that show Norumbega are little more than rough sketches of the seacoast. They indicate that the lost city was somewhere along the coast northeast of Virginia. Chesapeake Bay, the mouth of the Hudson River, the Boston area, and Penobscot Bay in Maine are among the sites proposed by scholars over the last two centuries or so. Yet there is another location that fits the description given by Jean Alfonse more precisely: the great island-dotted estuary of Narragansett Bay, where the Providence and Taunton Rivers flow into the Atlantic, one of the best natural harbors on the Atlantic coast. Certainly local folklore here in Rhode Island has long insisted that the lost city of Norumbega was located somewhere on Narragansett Bay's shores.

One other detail suggests that this may be the case. As mentioned above, an old map shows a "Fort Norumbega" located near the mouth of the estuary south of the city. A fortified watchtower in that location would have been valuable in the late sixteenth century, when Spanish fleets occasionally attacked other countries' settlements north of Spanish Florida. The mouth of Narragansett Bay has such a fortified watchtower: the Newport Tower itself, which is well positioned to watch the sea lanes approaching the bay. It is therefore worth considering the possibility the Newport Tower, whoever built it, may have been used by the Norumbegans to help keep Spanish raiders or pirates at bay.

None of this proves that Norumbega was in Rhode Island—or even that it existed at all. It shows only that such a city could have existed in the late sixteenth century, and that it might have been located in the area where Rhode Island folklore places it. Beyond this, at least at present, historical research is unable to go.

The investigation

If Norumbega existed somewhere toward the northern end of Narragansett Bay, and if (as suggested above) it was made of wood like most local Native communities, the last traces of the city will have been all but invisible by the time Providence Colony was founded in 1636. Now, after nearly four more centuries, any remaining physical traces will be buried deep, and their location cannot even be guessed. Under these circumstances psychic investigation is the only available option.

I made several attempts to reach Norumbega using scrying. Lacking any clear sense of its location, the name Norumbega was the focus I used. I made several attempts with mostly uncertain results. In the one vision I had that might have reached its target, I found myself on a pine-covered slope after sunset. The sky was still light to the west but the stars were visible across most of the sky, and a quarter moon shone down from above. I was facing south, down the slope toward the beach and the water. In the water were three tall ships at anchor with sails furled; I'm no specialist in maritime history but they had the high forecastles and sterns of the early Age of Exploration, not the flatter profile of ships of the types common after 1700.

All along the shore, stretching out at least half a mile along the water and going back from the beachfront to the beginning of the slope, were dwellings of various shapes. Some of them looked like illustrations I've seen of Native American houses in the Northeast; some looked like single-story medieval or Elizabethan English houses with wattle-and-daub (that is, clay plaster over twigs) walls; there were a few large structures, none of them more than a single story, that looked a little like someone had set out to make a medieval English barn but used sheets of bark, Native American style, for the roofs and walls. Firelight showed here and there, some of it from torches and lanterns being carried through the streets, some spilling out of doorways. Plenty of people milled around in the streets, but I couldn't see them clearly.

When I tried to walk down the slope toward the settlement, the vision broke up and I was not able to return to it. It remains an uncertain glimpse of something that might have been the fabled lost city of New England.

Sources

Baker et al. 1994; Horwitz 2008; Rauf 2019.

APPENDIX

Instructions for Practice

Seed thoughts

The seed thought at the beginning of each lesson sets the keynote for the lesson and for the week's work you will be putting into it. You will find it helpful to copy each seed thought, preferably by writing it out by hand on paper. Once you have copied it, post it someplace where you will see it several times in the course of each day. It is not necessary to set aside any special time to think about the seed thought. Like a seed, it will find the right place and time to take root, and bring you a harvest of unexpected insights.

If any of the seed thoughts strike you as especially interesting or inspiring, consider reading the book from which it is taken. The sources of all the seed thoughts in this book are included in the bibliography, and many of the books are easy to obtain.

Questions for reflection

These are meant to be used exactly as the phrase suggests. Like the seed thought for each lesson, the question for reflection is best copied out by hand and posted someplace where you will see it frequently.

Then, when you see it, ask yourself the question, and think about the answer. See whether your answer changes over the course of the week you spend on the lesson.

Discursive meditation

The kind of meditation practiced in traditional Western occult schools differs in an important way from the Eastern methods of meditation commonly practiced these days. Although there are exceptions, most Eastern methods of meditation work by turning off the objective mind. In some of these kinds of meditation, students learn to fix the attention on something other than thinking—a repeated mantra, a visualization, a cycle of breathing, or bare attention itself—so that their objective minds stop thinking altogether, and deeper patterns of awareness come to the fore. Others do the same thing in a subtler way, by teaching students to observe thoughts rising in the objective mind without actually thinking about them. Either of these can result in powerful spiritual experiences, but they have significant drawbacks. Shutting down the objective mind in this way too often produces people who have experienced deep spiritual states but have never learned how to think clearly, and often can't function well in everyday life.

The core traditions of Western meditation take a different path. Instead of stopping the thinking process, these methods point the focus of the objective mind on thinking itself, and turn the objective mind into a vehicle for spiritual awareness. In the standard Western method of meditation, this is done by focusing the mind on a specific topic, called a *theme*, and mentally following out the implications of that theme through a chain of ideas, all the while keeping the objective mind focused on the theme. With practice, the subjective mind joins in, and begins to hand the objective mind ideas and insights it wouldn't otherwise have had, so that meditation becomes a way for your two minds to work together.

This form of meditation is called *discursive meditation*, because it often takes the form of an inner discourse or dialogue. If you've practiced other kinds of meditation, discursive meditation will seem partly familiar to you and partly strange. If you've never meditated, the entire process will probably seem very strange to you! For that reason, it's best to learn discursive meditation a step at a time, beginning with posture.

To practice meditation you will need a place that is quiet and not too brightly lit. It should be private—a room with a door you can shut is best, though if you can't arrange that, a quiet corner and a little forbearance on the part of your housemates will do the job. You'll need a chair with a straight back, and a seat at a height that allows you to rest your feet flat on the floor while keeping your thighs level with the ground. You'll need a clock or watch, placed so that you can see it easily without moving your head. You'll also need this book, because the diagrams for each lesson are used in the meditation process. Once you have these simple preliminaries in place you are ready to begin.

One other detail is worth noting here. Many occult schools teach a basic ritual that is used to balance, energize, and cleanse the subtle body. In the Golden Section Fellowship, for example, the ritual used for this purpose is the Sphere of Protection. If the occult tradition you are studying includes such a ritual, it is a good idea to perform this before your meditation, so that you and the space you are in are both in a state of balance and clarity.

Posture

One of the benefits of discursive meditation is that you don't have to tie your legs into a knot to practice it. The posture to use is the one shown in any Egyptian statue of a seated god or goddess. Sit on a relatively hard chair. If it has a back, slide forward, so your back doesn't touch the chair's back at all. (This allows subtle energies to flow freely up and down your spine, which makes meditation easier.) Your feet should rest flat on the floor, your knees and hips are at right angles, your hands rest palm down on your thighs, and your head is straight. Keep your eyes open but relax your eyelids; look forward and down, as though at something on the floor a few yards ahead of you. Breathe slowly and easily.

When you're ready to practice, take this position, and don't move for five minutes. Don't fidget, shift, wiggle, scratch an itch or anything else. Leave your body completely still for five minutes by the clock. Do this once a day, preferably first thing in the morning, after your morning practice but before breakfast. Do this daily for one week.

Unless you've already done this, or practiced certain other exercises that have the same effect, this practice will be much harder than you think. Our bodies are actually full of tensions and discomforts we never notice, and part of the constant shifting and wiggling and fidgeting that most of us do most of the time is a matter of trying not to notice just how uncomfortable we are. Confront that evasion head on. Stay still for those five minutes, no matter what.

If you do that, you'll begin to learn one of the essential secrets of meditation. It is literally the most boring, grueling, frustrating thing you will ever do—and once you get the hang of how to do it and why it's important, you'll do it every day, because the benefits are worth the difficulties.

Relaxation

The second week's work is focused on relaxation. Most people these days realize that it's possible to be too tense. Since the opposite of one bad idea is generally another bad idea, it's worth remembering that it's also possible to be too relaxed. Until very recently, most people in Western societies were much too tense. It was extremely rare to encounter anyone in the Western world who was too relaxed, whose body was so lacking in tension that it was limp and floppy, and so teachers of spiritual exercises focused on relaxation. That had its effect, and now you find people on either end of the spectrum. What you find too rarely is people who have the balanced midpoint between too much tension and too much relaxation, which we can call poise.

The practice of sitting in a fixed and slightly unnatural posture is meant to keep you from being too relaxed. Keeping the spine straight, the head held up, the legs parallel, and the body still requires tension. Now we move to the other side of the balance and make sure you aren't too tense. This is done by relaxing your muscles while retaining the posture you've established. You don't move at all; you don't shift or wiggle or stretch; you just let go of the tensions you don't need to keep the posture.

Start at the crown of the head. Consciously relax any muscular tensions you find there. If you encounter a tension that won't let go, imagine that it is relaxing. (Your subjective mind will notice this, and the imagination will become reality with a little practice.) Spend a little while on that part of your body, and then move further down your head to the sides of the skull. Consciously relax any tensions you find there, if you can, and if you can't, imagine the tensions dissolving. Go all the way down your whole body this way, taking it a bit at a time, and doing the same twofold relaxation on each part of your body—consciously relax what you can, and imagine the rest letting go. This should take you at least five minutes, and quite possibly more than that. All the while, maintain the seated posture without moving. Don't pay attention to your breath—that's a later phase—or to anything outside yourself; simply focus on your body, and on the process by which you're releasing unnecessary tensions.

You may find that when you finish this, you ache from head to foot, or that some part of your body hurts a little—or a lot. That's what happens when you have a lot of unnecessary tension you stopped noticing a long time ago. With repeated practice, the tension will go away. You may also find that when you finish this, some of your muscles feel as though they've had a workout. They have—you've been holding your body in an unfamiliar position for a while, and that takes muscular effort. Your body will get used to that in due time.

This is the second stage of preparation for meditation: five minutes a day, sitting motionless in a chair, relaxing your unnecessary tensions. Do this for a week before going on to the next stage.

Breathing

How you breathe has powerful effects on your state of consciousness, and there are intricate systems of breathwork that take advantage of this for various purposes. If you don't have a teacher to supervise you and watch for signs of trouble, though, those can be risky. Breathwork stimulates the vagus nerve, a nerve that connects the vital organs with the brain, and so has a range of effects on your nervous system and your glands; if you do intensive breathwork without supervision, as a result, you can give yourself health problems.

Fortunately there are methods of breathwork that are safe to practice on your own, and one of them is very commonly used in occult meditation. It's called the Fourfold Breath. It's quite simple. You breathe in through your nose, slowly and deeply, to the count of four. You hold the breath in to the count of four. You breathe out through your nose, slowly and fully, to the count of four. You hold the breath out to the count of four. Repeat to the same steady rhythm.

How do you know how slow or fast to make the rhythm? Simply make it reasonably slow, but not so slow that you gasp or run out of air. Keep the movement of your breath steady, gentle, and flowing. No two people will have exactly the same rhythm, nor will you have the same rhythm every time you practice. Don't use a metronome or any other mechanical aid; just let yourself find a pace that works for you.

One detail worth noting is that you don't hold your breath by closing your throat; you hold it by keeping the muscles of your chest and abdomen in their positions, either expanded or relaxed. If you're used to closing your throat to hold your breath, it can take some practice to stop doing so. How do you tell if you're closing your throat? Draw in a deep breath, hold it for a little while, and then breathe out. If you hear or feel a little "pop" inside your throat, you've closed it. To keep from doing that, keep trying to breathe in a trickle of air while you hold your breath in, and keep trying to breathe out a trickle of air when you're holding your breath out. You'll get the hang of it quickly.

For the next week, five minutes of the Fourfold Breath will be your practice. Take the position, hold yourself still, and let the tension drain away from the crown of your head to the soles of your feet, just as you did last week. Take a minute or two to do this, then begin the Fourfold Breath. Keep doing it for five minutes by the clock. This is the sequence you'll use to begin the process of meditation for real next week. Keep at it, and see where it takes you.

Meditation

So far we've dealt with posture, relaxation, and breathing: the preliminaries to discursive meditation. Now it's time to go all the way and meditate. To make sense of what follows, it's important to remember that the word "meditation" literally means "thinking." (That's why we use the word "premeditated" for a crime that the perpetrator thought about before committing.) Your task in meditation is to think deliberately, seriously, and intentionally about a theme. While you work with the material in this book, the themes for your meditation are the seven paragraphs given for each lesson.

When you're ready to begin meditation, set up the diagram for the lesson you're studying so you can see it clearly from your meditation chair without turning your head. Sit down in the position we've discussed and settle into it, neither tense nor relaxed but poised. Let go of excess tension, beginning from the top of your head and letting it drain down from there; spend about a minute at that. Then do five minutes of the Fourfold Breath, letting your mind focus solely on your breathing. At this point you're ready to begin.

Spend a few moments looking at the diagram for the lesson, and then call to mind the paragraph on which you're going to meditate. Recall it as clearly as you can. Hold it in your mind for a little while, and then begin thinking about it.

As you do so, your thoughts will wander off the theme. Bring them back. They'll wander off again. Bring them back again. You'll have as much trouble keeping your mind on the theme as the practitioner of mind-emptying styles of meditation has keeping thoughts at bay, and you'll develop the same skills of catching your mind wandering and bringing it back to the subject of the meditation. In the intervals between these vagaries, on the other hand, you'll be learning something about the theme, and you'll also be working on the capacity for focused reflective thought, an essential human skill and one very poorly developed by most of us. Keep working on the theme for ten minutes by the clock. When you are finished, take a deep breath or two and then go on with the rest of your day.

Scrying

In Western occult teachings, discursive meditation is paired with another meditative exercise, which is called scrying. Scrying originally meant seeing in the ordinary sense—the word "descry," meaning "to see something at a distance," still gets a little use in poetry and literature—but the word was adopted centuries ago by occultists for a very special kind of seeing that doesn't rely on the physical eyes.

Scrying works with your imagination in much the same way that discursive meditation works with your thoughts. To scry, you start with a *portal image*, which serves the same function as the theme does in discursive meditation. A portal image combines two symbols—the first is a symbol that lets your subjective mind know you're turning your attention to associations on the astral plane, the second is the specific symbol you want to use to draw associations to you. Standard occult practice for many years has been to use the image of a doorway for the first, and to put the second symbol on the doorway as though it's painted or carved there.

You use the same posture and preliminary steps for scrying that you use for meditation. Sit down in the posture, relax your material body from head to toe, and spend five minutes doing the Fourfold Breath. If you pray at this point in your meditation, do exactly the same thing when scrying. Once you're ready, imagine the portal image in front of you: a door with the symbol you've chosen painted or carved on it.

Once you've built up the portal image as clearly as you can, imagine the door swinging slowly open. Beyond it is a landscape of some sort. Don't decide what it looks like in advance. Let it be whatever comes into your mind, and spend a minute or more letting it take shape in your imagination before going on. Then, slowly and clearly, imagine yourself getting up out of your chair, walking up to the doorway, and going through it. The door remains open behind you, and if you look back you can see your physical body sitting in the chair. Look around at the realm beyond the door, and notice as many details as you can.

For your first few experiments in scrying, this is as much as you need to do. Once you're familiar with the practice you can go further. The best way to do this is to call for a guide. As you stand there in the imaginary landscape beyond the door, imagine yourself saying aloud, "In the name of the Eternal Spiritual Sun I ask that a true and faithful guide be sent to me." (If you are a religious person you can use the name of a Deity in place of the reference to the Eternal Spiritual Sun.) Then, imagine a guide coming to you. Don't decide in advance who or what the guide will be. Let it be whatever appears in your imagination at that moment. It may take human, animal, or some other form.

Whatever its form, ask it whether it comes in the name of the Eternal Spiritual Sun (or the name of the Deity if you've used that instead.) Talk with it, and ask it to show you some of the secrets of whatever symbol it is you put into the portal image. Your guide will most likely take you on a journey through the imaginary landscape beyond the portal image, showing you things that reveal something of the inner meaning of the symbol, and it may also instruct you directly. Ask it any questions you wish, and pay close attention to its answers. Every detail of the landscape around you and every word spoken to you has something to teach. Treat the things you encounter as though they were real, for as long as the scrying lasts.

A certain degree of caution is in order when dealing with the guide and the other beings you may encounter in the imaginary space beyond the portal image. Some of these are honest and will teach you worthwhile things, but others may try to deceive you. Some people find it hard to think of imaginary beings in these terms, but the metaphor of the screen with two projectors should be kept in mind here. Imaginary beings can be as independent of the scryer's will as the people who appear in dreams; they have a life of their own, and can behave in unexpected ways. Treat them with the same courtesy and caution you would use toward strangers in an unfamiliar town.

When the journey or the instruction comes to an end, ask your guide to bring you back to your starting point, thank it for its guidance and bless it in the name of the Eternal Spiritual Sun or the name of the Deity you invoked earlier. Then return through the doorway, imagine yourself sitting back in the chair where your physical body has been all the while, and then slowly and carefully imagine the door closing. As it closes, concentrate on the thought that no unwanted energies or beings can come into your daily life from the realm you've been scrying. Use a few cycles of fourfold breath to clear your mind, then close just as you would at the end of a session of meditation, complete with self-massage. Write up the experience in your practice journal as soon as possible, while the details are still fresh in your mind.

You may find yourself a little disoriented at first after scrying, especially the first few times you do it. If so, eating some food will help refocus your attention on your body and the material plane of existence. Routine activities such as washing the dishes can also help reorient your awareness back to the realm of ordinary experience.

Working with scrying

As already noted, scrying is a kind of meditation that works with your imagination rather than your thoughts. Once you've become comfortable with discursive meditation, you can start using scrying now and then in place of your regular discursive meditation. The images and ideas you get from your scrying then become themes for discursive meditations in the days that follow. For every day you practice scrying, plan on spending at least three days, and maybe more, using discursive meditation to make sense of the meaning of the things you saw and heard during the scrying. For example, you can look back over the entry in your practice journal and sort out what you encountered into events, symbols, and information, and then devote one session of meditation to each of these.

As you meditate on the images, remember that there are no right answers and no wrong answers. The goal of this exercise is not to come up with some set of standardized result, but to teach your objective mind to be attentive to symbols, to think with them, to get a sense of the things they can mean and the things they mean to you personally. Feel free, when meditating on the results of a scrying, to draw on your own memories and inner life as a resource. Does the meadow you see while scrying remind you of a place you visited in childhood, for example, and what does that memory suggest to you?

That said, not everything in a scrying is necessarily a fount of wisdom. One problem faced by beginners in scrying, especially those who don't have a lot of prior experience with meditation, is that stray thoughts and irrelevancies end up being woven into the scrying by the half-trained mind. Like a radio symbol in which the message is mixed with static, scryings by novice scryers often contain a mix of useful material and random imagery. As you meditate on each scrying, keep an eye out for things that seem clearly out of place.

Scrying can be a powerful tool for deepening your understanding of symbols and opening up the hidden potentials of human awareness, but it can also be an opportunity for many different kinds of foolishness, some of them relatively amusing, some a good deal less so. People have made spectacular blunders by blindly trusting information received from scrying and similar practices. The best way to avoid these pitfalls is to remember that scryings take place on the astral plane, the realm of dreams and imagination, and the information you receive in them may or may not have anything to do with the material plane where most of us live most of our lives. Common sense is just as important in occultism as it is in the rest of life!

BIBLIOGRAPHY

Anonymous, "Cow, Monster, or Ghost? Reappearance of the Fearsome Thing that Pirate Hicks Discovered Fifty Years Ago," *The Evening Hour*, 15 January 1896.

Arnold, Neil, "The Glocester Ghoul," *Cryptozoology Online*, http://forte-anzoology.blogspot.com/2010/04/neil-arnold-glocester-ghoul.html, accessed 26 December 2022.

Baker, Emerson W., Edwin A. Churchill, Richard S. D'Abato, Kristine L. Jones, Victor A. Konrad, and Harald E. L. Prins, *American Beginnings: Exploration, Culture, and Cartography in the Land of Norumbega* (Lincoln, NE: University of Nebraska Press, 1994).

Blackstone, Nathaniel Brewster, *The Biography of the Reverend William Blackstone* (Homestead, FL: The author, 1974).

Bord, Janet, *Fairies: Real Encounters with Little People* (New York: Dell, 1997).

Bord, Janet, and Colin, *Alien Animals* (London: Grafton, 1980).

Brandon, Jim, *The Rebirth of Pan: Hidden Faces of the American Earth Spirit* (Dunlap, IL: Firebird, 1983).

Brandon, Jim, *Weird America* (New York: Dutton, 1978).

Briggs, Katharine M., *An Encyclopedia of Fairies* (New York: Pantheon, 1976.)

Briggs, Katharine M., *The Anatomy of Puck* (London: Routledge & Kegan Paul, 1959).

Briggs, Katharine M., *The Vanishing People* (London: Batsford, 1978).
Brigham, Herbert Olin, *The Old Stone Mill* (Newport, RI: Franklin Printing House, 1948).
Brunvand, Jan Harold, *The Vanishing Hitchhiker: American Urban Legends and Their Meanings* (New York: W. W. Norton, 1981).
Butler, W. E., *How to Read the Aura, Practice Psychometry, Telepathy and Clairvoyance* (Rochester, VT: Destiny, 1987).
Clark, Jerome, and Loren Coleman, *Creatures of the Outer Edge* (New York: Warner, 1978).
Coleman, Loren, *Curious Encounters* (Boston, MA: Faber & Faber, 1985).
Coleman, Loren, *Mysterious America* (Boston, MA: Faber & Faber, 1983).
Corliss, William R., *Ancient Man: A Handbook of Puzzling Artifacts* (Glen Arm, MD: The Sourcebook Project, 1978).
Critchlow, Keith, *Time Stands Still: New Light on Megalithic Science* (New York: St. Martins, 1982).
Crombie, R. Ogilvie, *Encounters with Nature Spirits: Co-Creating with the Elemental Kingdom* (Rochester, VT: Findhorn Press, 2009).
Curran, Douglas, *In Advance of the Landing: Folk Concepts of Outer Space* (New York: Abbeville Press, 1985).
Da Silva, Dr. Manuel Luciano, *Portuguese Pilgrims and Dighton Rock* (Bristol, RI: By the author, 1971).
Devereux, Paul, *Earth Lights* (Wellingborough, UK: Turnstone, 1982)
Devereux, Paul, *Earth Lights Revelation* (London: Blandford, 1990).
Devereux, Paul, *Earth Memory* (St. Paul, MN: Llewellyn, 1992).
Devereux, Paul, *Places of Power* (London: Blandford, 1990).
Devereux, Paul, *Shamanism and the Mystery Lines* (St. Paul, MN: Llewellyn, 1993).
Devereux, Paul, and Ian Thomson, *The Ley Hunter's Companion* (London: Thames & Hudson, 1979).
Eberhart, George M., *A Geo-Bibliography of Anomalies* (Westport, CT: Greenwood, 1980).
Eberhart, George M., *Monsters: A Guide to Information on Unaccounted-for Creatures, Including Bigfoot, Many Water Monsters, and Other Irregular Animals* (New York: Garland, 1983).
Egan, James Alan, *Elizabethan America* (Newport, RI: Cosmopolite Press, 2011).
Eitel, Ernest J., *Feng Shui* (Hong Kong: Trubner, 1873).
Eliade, Mircea, *Cosmos and History: The Myth of the Eternal Return* (New York: Harper, 1959).
Fidler, J. Havelock, *Ley Lines: Their Nature and Properties* (Wellingborough, UK: Turnstone, 1983).
Fort, Charles, *The Complete Books of Charles Fort* (New York: Dover, 1974).

Fortune, Dion, *Applied Magic* and *Aspects of Occultism* (Wellingborough, UK: Aquarian, 1987).
Fortune, Dion, *Esoteric Orders and their Work* and *The Training and Work of the Initiate* (Wellingborough, UK: Aquarian, 1987).
Fortune, Dion, *The Goat Foot God* (York Beach, ME: Weiser, 1980).
Fortune, Dion, Margaret Lumley Brown, and Gareth Knight, *The Arthurian Formula* (Loughborough, UK: Thoth, 2006).
Girard, Michael, "The Glocester Ghoul," *Strange New England*, http://strange-new-england.com/2017/10/22/the-glocester-ghoul/, accessed 26 December 2022.
Godfrey, Linda S., *American Monsters* (New York: Tarcher, 2014).
Godfrey, Linda S., *Monsters Among Us* (New York: Tarcher, 2016).
Godfrey, Linda S., *Real Wolfmen: True Encounters in Modern America* (New York: Tarcher, 2012).
Graves, Tom, *The Diviner's Handbook: A Guide to the Timeless Art of Dowsing* (Rochester, VT: Destiny, 1990).
Graves, Tom, *Needles of Stone* (London: Turnstone, 1978).
Graves, Tom, and Liz Poraj-Wilczynska, *The Disciplines of Dowsing* (Colchester, UK: Tetradian, 2008).
Greer, John Michael, *Monsters* (London: Aeon, 2019).
Greer, John Michael, *The UFO Chronicles* (London: Aeon, 2020)
Greer, John Michael, *The Way of the Golden Section* (London: Aeon, 2021).
Harpur, Patrick, *Daimonic Reality: A Field Guide to the Otherworld* (New York: Viking, 1994).
Hauck, Dennis William, *Haunted Places: The National Directory* (New York: Penguin, 1996).
Hesse, Hermann, *The Glass Bead Game*, trans. Richard and Clara Winston (New York: Holt, Rinehart & Winston, 1969).
Heuvelmans, Bernard, *In the Wake of the Sea Serpent* (New York: Hill and Wang, 1968).
Heuvelmans, Bernard, *On the Track of Unknown Animals* (London: Kegan Paul, 1955)
Holiday, F. W., *The Dragon and the Disc: An Investigation into the Totally Fantastic* (New York: W. W. Norton, 1973).
Horwitz, Tony, *A Voyage Long and Strange: Rediscovering the New World* (New York: Henry Holt, 2008).
Hufford, David, *The Terror That Comes in the Night* (Philadelphia, PA: University of Pennsylvania Press, 1982).
Jung, C. G., *The Archetypes and the Collective Unconscious*, trans. R. F. C. Hull (Princeton, NJ: Princeton University Press, 1968).
Jung, C. G., *Civilization in Transition*, trans. R. F. C. Hull (Princeton, NJ: Princeton University Press, 1964).

Jung, C. G., *Flying Saucers: A Modern Myth of Things Seen in the Sky*, trans. R. F. C. Hull (Princeton, NJ: Princeton University Press, 1978).
Jung, C. G., *Man and His Symbols* (New York: Doubleday, 1964).
Jung, C. G., *Memories, Dreams, Reflections* (New York: Random House, 1961).
Keel, John, *The Mothman Prophecies* (New York: Tor, 1991).
Keel, John, *Operation Trojan Horse* (San Antonio, TX: Anomalist, 2013).
Keel, John, *Strange Creatures from Time and Space* (Point Pleasant, WV: Saucerian, 2014).
Knight, Gareth, *Dion Fortune's Rites of Isis and of Pan* (Cheltenham, UK: Skylight, 2013).
Kreisberg, Glenn, *Spirits in Stone: The Secrets of Megalithic America* (Rochester, VT: Bear & Co., 2018).
Landau, Misia, *Narratives of Human Evolution* (New Haven, CT: Yale University Press, 1991).
Lethbridge, T. C., *The Essential T. C. Lethbridge*, ed. Tom Graves and Janet Hoult (London: Routledge & Kegan Paul, 1980).
Lethbridge, T. C., *Ghost and Divining-Rod* (London: Routledge & Kegan Paul, 1963).
Lethbridge, T. C., *Ghost and Ghoul* (London: Routledge & Kegan Paul, 1961).
Lethbridge, T. C., *The Power of the Pendulum* (London: Arkana, 1984).
Lind, Louise, *William Blackstone: Sage of the Wilderness* (Bowie, MD: Heritage Books, 1993).
Mackal, Roy P., *Searching for Hidden Animals* (Garden City, NY: Doubleday, 1980).
McClenon, James, *Deviant Science: The Case of Parapsychology* (Philadelphia, PA: University of Pennsylvania Press, 1984).
Michell, John, *A Little History of Astro-Archaeology* (London: Thames & Hudson, 1989).
Michell, John, *City of Revelation* (New York: David McKay, 1972).
Michell, John, *The Dimensions of Paradise* (London: Thames & Hudson, 1988).
Michell, John, *The Earth Spirit: Its Ways, Shrines and Mysteries* (New York: Crossroad, 1975).
Michell, John, *The New View Over Atlantis* (London: Thames & Hudson, 1983).
Michell, John, *The View Over Atlantis* (New York: Ballantine, 1969).
Michell, John, and Christine Rhone, *Twelve-Tribe Nations and the Ancient Science of Enchanting the Landscape* (London: Thames & Hudson, 1991).
Morris, William, *The Well at the World's End* (New York: Ballantine, 1970).
Nichols, Ross, "An Examination of Creative Myth," in Nichols, Ross, and James Kirkup, *The Cosmic Shape* (London: Forge Press, 1946).
Nichols, Ross, *The Book of Druidry* (London: Aquarian, 1990).
Ocker, J. W., *The United States of Cryptids* (Philadelphia, PA: Quirk, 2022).

Pennick, Nigel, *The Ancient Science of Geomancy* (London: Thames & Hudson, 1979).
Pennick, Nigel, *Creating Places of Power* (Rochester, VT: Inner Traditions, 2022).
Pennick, Nigel, *Earth Harmony* (London: Century, 1987).
Pennick, Nigel, *Games of the Gods* (York Beach, ME: Weiser, 1989).
Pennick, Nigel, *Sacred Geometry* (Wellingborough, UK: Turnstone, 1980).
Pennick, Nigel, and Paul Devereux, *Lines on the Landscape* (London: Hale, 1989).
Persinger, Michael A., and Gyslaine F. Lafreniere, *Space-Time Transients and Unusual Events* (Chicago, IL: Nelson-Hall, 1977).
Rauf, Don, *Lost America* (Lanham, MD: Globe Pequot, 2019).
Rhode's Gallery (pseudonym), "The Hermit of Study Hill. Where are Blackstone's Bones?" *Rhode's Gallery* (http://rhodesgallery.home.blog/2018/10/17/the-hermit-of-study-hill-where-are-reverand-blackstones-bones/, accessed 11 September 2022).
Rosney, Mark, Rob Bethell, and Jebby Robinson, *A Beginner's Guide to Paranormal Investigation* (Stroud, UK: Amberley, 2009)
Shuker, Dr. Karl P. N., *From Flying Toads to Snakes with Wings* (St. Paul, MN: Llewellyn, 1997).
Spence, Lewis, *The Minor Traditions of British Mythology* (New York: Arno Press, 1979).
Taylor, Troy, *The Ghost Hunter's Guidebook* (Decatur, IL: Whitechapel, 2007).
Thompson, Keith, *Angels and Aliens: UFOs and the Mythic Imagination* (New York: Addison Wesley, 1991).
Tolkien, J. R. R., *The Two Towers* (New York: Ballantine, 1965).
Trento, Salvatore Michael, *The Search for Lost America: The Mysteries of the Stone Ruins in the United States* (New York: Penguin, 1978).
Underwood, Guy, *The Pattern of the Past* (New York: Abelard-Schumann, 1973).
Vallee, Jacques, *Messengers of Deception: UFO Contacts and Cults* (Berkeley, CA: And/Or Press, 1979).
Vallee, Jacques, *Passport to Magonia* (Chicago, IL: Henry Regnery, 1969).
Watkins, Alfred, *Early British Trackways* (London: Simpkin, Marshall, Hamilton, Kent, & Co. 1922).
Watkins, Alfred, *The Ley Hunter's Manual* (Wellingborough, UK: Turnstone, 1983).
Watkins, Alfred, *The Old Straight Track* (London: Methuen, 1925).
Ziarek, Ewa, *An Ethics of Dissensus* (Stanford, CA: Stanford University Press, 2001).

INDEX

ABCs (anomalous black cats), 166.
    See also animals, mysterious
abominable snowman, 170. *See also*
    hominids, mysterious
alignments
    celestial alignments, 85–87
    leys, 77–79
    relics out of place, 89–91
    spirit roads, 81–83
ancient and mysterious sites, 53
    mystical trail, 53–55
    myths and legends, 54
    orientation, 53–55
    phenomena, 55
    practical work, 55
    question for reflection, 55
    role of sites in earth mysteries, 57
    Seen and the Unseen, 54
    supernatural connections, 53–55
ancient scripts, 97–98. *See also* language
    of the land
ancient spiritual traditions, 83
animals, mysterious, 165

    anomalous black cats, 166
    black dogs of England's west
        country, 166
    cryptozoology, 166
    Hound of the Baskervilles, The, 166
    orientation, 165–167
    practical work, 167
    question for reflection, 167
    unknown animals and mysterious
        creatures, 165–167
anomalous black cats. *See* ABCs
appearances and disappearances, 177
    orientation, 177–179
    practical work, 179
    question for reflection, 179
archetype, 115. *See also* myth
    collective unconscious, 116
    Man and His Symbols, 117
    narratives in contemporary
        consciousness, 123–125
    orientation, 115–117
    power of, 115–117
    power of beginnings, 127–129

INDEX

practical work, 117
question for reflection, 117
Wise Old Man, 116
A True Discourse of the Adventures and Travailes of David Ingram, 224
Aubrey, John, 44

ball lightning, 186. *See also* earth lights
BHMs (big hairy monsters), 169. *See also* hominids, mysterious
big hairy monsters. *See* BHMs
black dogs of England's west country, 166. *See also* animals, mysterious
Blackstone and Yellow Sweeting apple, 205
Buchanan, Joseph Rodes, 31

celestial alignments, 85–87. *See also* earth and heavens
chalk figures of England, 66–67. *See also* mounds and earthworks
chupacabra (goat vampire), 174. *See also* creatures, impossible
church roads. *See* spirit roads
clusters and connections, 193
  flap, 194
  orientation, 193–195
  paranormal phenomena, 193
  practical work, 195
  question for reflection, 195
  windows, 194
collective unconscious, 116, 120, 121. *See also* archetype
consensus, 44
continental drift, 212
corpse roads. *See* spirit roads
creation myths, 127–129
  pairing of man and bull, 204
creatures, impossible, 173
  chupacabra (goat vampire), 174
  exploring impossibilities and collective imagination, 173–175
  Jersey Devil, 174
  orientation, 173–175

"Oz Factor, the", 174
practical work, 175
question for reflection, 175
realm of paranormal cryptids, 173–175
creatures, mysterious, 209
cromlech, 70. *See also* megaliths
cryptids, paranormal, 173–175. *See also* creatures, impossible
cryptozoology, 166. *See also* animals, mysterious
  anomalous black cats, 166
  black dogs of England's west country, 166
  Gigantopithecus, 170
  Hound of the Baskervilles, The, 166
culture's beliefs, 89

date of origin, 74
dead ways. *See* spirit roads
descry, 235. *See also* scrying
"dirt time", xii
discursive meditation, 23–25, 230. *See also* scrying
  breathing, 233–234
  Fourfold Breath, 233, 234
  meditation, 234–235
  posture, 231–232
  relaxation, 232–233
disenchanted state, 16
disenchantment and conventional wisdom, 143–145
disenchantment of world, 11
  act of reawakening to enchantment, 13
  disenchantment, 12
  enchantment, 13
  eras of enchantment, 12
  orientation, 11–13
  practical work, 13
  question for reflection, 13
  rediscovering magic, consciousness, and life, 11–13
  time of disenchantment, 12
dissensus, 44
dogma of materialism, 7, 112

dolmen/cromlech, 70. *See also* megaliths
dowsing, 27
   dowser device, 28
   orientation, 27–29
   practical work, 29
   question for reflection, 29
   tapping into the Unseen for earth mysteries exploration, 27–29
   training, 29

earth and heavens, 85
   celestial alignments, 85–87
   exploring heavenly mysteries of ancient sites, 85–87
   orientation, 85–87
   practical work, 87
   question for reflection, 87
earth currents, 57
   blue dragon and white tiger, 58
   feng shui, 58–59
   orientation, 57–59
   practical work, 59
   question for reflection, 59
   Unseen in landscape, 57
earth lights, 185. *See also* unidentified flying objects
   ball lightning, 186
   earthquake lights, 186
   light phenomena, 186
   magnetic "hot spots", 186–187
   orientation, 185–187
   practical work, 187
   question for reflection, 187
   swamp lights, 186
earthquake lights, 186. *See also* earth lights
earth's mysteries, ix
   explorations and investigations in local region, 202
   exploring hidden dimensions of, 7–9
   myth, legend, and history in landscape of, 131–133
   occult study and earth mysteries research, x–xi

Ovate Grade correspondence course, xiii
   researchers, xi–xii
   in search of, 47–49
   sites of interest to, 54
   study and fieldwork, xi–xiii
   unraveling strange events, 135–137
   View Over Atlantis, The, xiii
earthworks. *See* mounds and earthworks
Eastern methods of meditation, 230
Egan, Jim, 219
enchantment, 12, 13. *See also* disenchantment of world
   maps, 149
   of wipes, 143–145
erratics, 70. *See also* megaliths
esoteric science, 19
exoteric science, 19
exploration, 202
   Glocester dragon, 209–213
   legend of William Blackstone, 203–207
   lost city of Norumbega, 223–228
   Newport Tower, 215–221

feng shui, 58–59
flap, 194. *See also* clusters and connections
Flying Saucers: A Modern Myth of Things Seen in the Sky, 191
Fort, Charles, 178, 209
Fort Norumbega, 227. *See also* Norumbega, lost city of
Fourfold Breath, 233, 234. *See also* discursive meditation

ghosts and haunting, 161
   orientation, 161–163
   paranormal phenomena and hidden realities, 161–163
   poltergeist, 162
   practical work, 163
   question for reflection, 163
ghosts, individual, 209
ghoul, 211

Gigantopithecus, 170. *See also* hominids, mysterious
Glocester dragon, 209
 continental drift, 212
 directions to Glocester dragon territory, 213
 discussion, 211–213
 evidence, 210–211
 investigation, 213
 localized creatures, 209
Glocester Ghoul, 211
glyphs, 66–67. *See also* mounds and earthworks
goat vampire. See *chupacabra*
gods and goddesses, x
Golden Section Fellowship, x, 23, 231

haymow, 217
historical landscape, 107
 exploring landscape of narratives, 107–109
 history, 107–108
 history as storytelling, 107–109
 orientation, 107–109
 practical work, 109
 question for reflection, 109
history, 104, 107–108. *See also* stories
 history and myth, 119
 myth, legend, and, 131–133
 pseudohistory, 108
 realms of, 131
 as storytelling, 107–109
hominids, mysterious, 169
 big hairy monsters, 169
 Gigantopithecus, 170
 local monster lore, 171
 orientation, 169–171
 practical work, 171
 question for reflection, 171
 Yeti, 170
Hound of the Baskervilles, The, 166. *See also* animals, mysterious
Hufford, David, 136

individual ghosts, 209
Indo-European mythologies, 204

industrial societies
 belief in, 90
 narratives about future, 140
 rejection of the Unseen, 136
 stories, 104
inner sense development, 23
 discursive meditation, 23–25
 orientation, 23–25
 practical work, 25
 question for reflection, 25
 scrying, 23–25
inner senses, 19
 embracing dual perception, 19–21
 imagination, 20
 orientation, 19–21
 practical work, 21
 psychometry, 32–33
 question for reflection, 21
 uniting the Seen and the Unseen, 19–21
instructions for practice, 229
 discursive meditation, 230–235
 questions for reflection, 229–230
 scrying, 235–238
 seed thoughts, 229
investigations, conducting, 202
 Glocester dragon, 209–213
 legend of William Blackstone, 203–207
 lost city of Norumbega, 223–228
 Newport Tower, 215–221

Jersey Devil, 174, 209. *See also* creatures, impossible
Johnny Appleseed, 205, 207
Jung, Carl, 115, 191. *See also* archetype

King Arthur, 47, 132, 205

land as palimpsest, 61
 forces of nature, 62
 layers of "writing", 62
 orientation, 61–63
 practical work, 63
 question for reflection, 63
 unveiling the layers, 61–63

landscape patterns, 93
  landscape zodiac, 94
  ley research, 94
  orientation, 93–95
  practical work, 95
  question for reflection, 95
  Stukeley's serpent, 93–94, 95
  tracing ancient traces and
      speculative interpretations,
      93–95
landscape zodiac, 94
language of the land, 97
  decipherment of ancient scripts, 98
  Newport Tower in Rhode Island, 98
  orientation, 97–99
  patience and open-mindedness,
      97–99
  practical work, 99
  question for reflection, 99
  unknown ancient script, 97–98
Laudau, Misia, 128
legend(s), 104. *See also* stories
  of beginnings, 127
  categories, 120
  future in, 139–141
  myth, legend, and history, 131–133
  realms of, 131
legendary landscape, 119
legends of past, 119
  collective unconscious, 120–121
  gigantic lumberman Paul
      Bunyan, 120
  history and myth, 119
  Johnny Appleseed, 120
  King Richard the Lionhearted, 120
  orientation, 119–121
  practical work, 121
  question for reflection, 121
  Robin Hood, 120
legends of present, 123
  archetypal narratives in
      contemporary consciousness,
      123–125
  earth mysteries research, 124–125
  orientation, 123–125
  practical work, 125

question for reflection, 125
  urban legends, 124
ley lines. *See* leys
leys, 77
  ancient pathways and mysterious
      energies, 77–79
  ley lines enigma, 77–79
  ley walking, 79
  Old Straight Track, The, 78
  orientation, 77–79
  practical work, 79
  question for reflection, 79
light phenomena, 186. *See also* earth
      lights
localized creatures, 209
local monster lore, 171. *See also*
      hominids, mysterious

magic presence in sacred places, 3
  orientation, 3–5
  practical work, 5
  question for reflection, 5
  studies, 4
magnetic "hot spots", 186–187. *See also*
      earth lights
Maltwood, Katharine, 94
Man and His Symbols, 117
"map is not the territory, The", 158
materialist dogmas, 44
megaliths, 69
  dolmen/cromlech, 70
  erratics, 70
  etymology, 69
  menhir, 70
  orientation, 69–71
  practical work, 71
  question for reflection, 71
  supernatural experiences, 71
  trilithon, 70
menhir, 70. *See also* megaliths
Menzies, Gavin, 218
Merlin. *See* Myrddin Wyllt
mounds and earthworks, 65
  categories, 66
  chalk figures of England, 66–67
  enclosures, 66

250 INDEX

glyphs, 66–67
Nazca plain in Peru, 67
orientation, 65–67
practical work, 67
question for reflection, 67
Myrddin Wyllt ("wild Merlin"), 205
mysterious phenomenon, studying, 49
myth, 104, 111. *See also* stories
  of ancient Persia, 204
  and archetypes, 115–117
  barrier to understanding, 112
  creation myths, 127–129
  etymology, 111–112
  future in, 139–141
  history and, 119
  Indo-European mythologies, 204
  myth, legend, and history, 131–133
  Norse mythology, 204
  occultists, 112
  pairing of man and bull, 204
  power and importance of, 111–113
  realms of, 131
mythic landscape, 111
  insights into inner dimensions of land, 111–113
  myths, 111
  orientation, 111–113
  practical work, 113
  question for reflection, 113
  storytelling, 113

narrative landscape, 147
  orientation, 147–149
  parts of, 148
  practical work, 149
  question for reflection, 149
  stories and meaning in the land, 147–149
Narratives of Human Evolution, 128
natural philosophers, 44
natural philosophy, 43
  advantage of, 45
  awareness, 43
  consensus, 44
  dissensus, 44
  embracing dissensus, 43–45
  materialist dogmas, 44
  orientation, 43–45
  practical work, 45
  question for reflection, 45
  science vs., 44
  scientists, 43–44
nature, attuning to, 35. *See* sensory awareness
Nazca plain in Peru, 67. *See also* mounds and earthworks
Newport Tower, 98, 215
  directions to Touro Park, 221
  discussion, 217–220
  evidence, 215–217
  investigation, 220–221
Norse mythology, 204
Norumbega, lost city of, 223
  context, 225–227
  evidence, 223–225
  Fort Norumbega, 227
  investigation, 227–228
  location, 226–227
  True Discourse of the Adventures and Travailes of David Ingram, A, 224

OBOD. *See* Order of Bards Ovates and Druids
occulta philosophia, x
occultism, x
  basic elements of occult theory, 7–8
  occultists, 7
  occult perspective on aerial apparitions, 48–49
  occult teachings, 8
  principle of, 8
occultist, 7, 48
  myths, 112
occult, x
  arts, 199
  and earth mysteries research, x–xi
  Golden Section Fellowship, x
  philosophy, 199
  study, x
  teachings, 8
  theory, 7–8
Old Straight Track, The, 78

INDEX   251

Order of Bards Ovates and Druids
    (OBOD), xiii
outer senses, 35
out-of-place artifacts. *See* relics out
    of place
"Oz Factor, the", 174. *See also* creatures,
    impossible

palimpsest, 61
paranormal. *See also* clusters and
    connections; creatures,
    impossible; ghosts and
    haunting
  cryptids, 173–175
  events, 136
  hidden realities, 161–163
  phenomena, 193
phantasmagoria, 159
phantasmagoria factor, 157
  "map is not the territory,
    The", 158
  navigating the map and territory,
    157–159
  orientation, 157–159
  practical work, 159
  question for reflection, 159
  research into unexplained
    phenomena, 158
  understanding earth mysteries
    and unexplained phenomena,
    157–159
phenomena, 153, 198
  basic principles, 154
  encountering the unexplained,
    153–155
  orientation, 153–155
  and place, 154–155
  practical work, 155
  question for reflection, 155
  UFO phenomenon, 154
  "windows", 154
poltergeist, 162. *See also* ghosts
    and haunting
pseudohistory, 108
pseudoskeptics, 144
psychometry, 31
  application, 32–33

classic psychometric training, 32
  orientation, 31–33
  practical work, 33
  question for reflection, 33
realm of the unknown, 47
  being an occultist, 48
  occult perspective on aerial
    apparitions, 48–49
  orientation, 47–49
  practical work, 49
  question for reflection, 49
  studying mysterious
    phenomenon, 49
reenchantment of the world, 15
  disenchanted state, 16
  healing ourselves and world, 15–17
  orientation, 15–17
  practical work, 17
  question for reflection, 17
  rediscovery of magic, 17
relics out of place, 89
  belief in industrial societies, 90
  challenging conventional history
    of humanity, 89–91
  culture's beliefs, 89
  orientation, 89–91
  practical work, 91
  question for reflection, 91
  unveiling ancient mysteries,
    89–91
Rhode Island, 203, 204
  Glocester dragon, 209–213
  legend of William Blackstone
    203–207
  Newport Tower, 215–221
  Western, 213
Rhode Island's Stonehenge.
    See Newport Tower
Rollright Stones, 132

sacred places, 73
  date of origin, 74
  mapping out geography
    of Unseen, 74
  orientation, 73–75
  practical work, 75
  question for reflection, 75

252 INDEX

sacred structures and earth
    energies, 73–75
    unveiling the power of place, 73–75
science, 44
scientists, 43–44
scripts, ancient, 97–98. *See also*
    language of the land
scrying, 23–25, 235. *See also* discursive
    meditation
    descry, 235
    working with, 237–238
seasonal cycles, 39
    orientation, 39–41
    phenomena, 40
    practical work, 41
    question for reflection, 41
    secrets of nature and ancient
        wisdom, 39–41
    stories, 40
Seen and the Unseen, 7, 19, 36, 49, 54, 197
    difference between, 199
    exploring hidden dimensions
        of earth mysteries, 7–9
    orientation, 7–9, 197–199
    phenomena, 198
    practical work, 9, 199
    question for reflection, 9, 199
    sites, stories, and phenomena,
        197–199
    stories, 198
    Unseen, 8
Seen, the, 19
sensory awareness, 35
    developing sensory awareness,
        35–37
    orientation, 35–37
    outer senses, 35
    practical work, 37
    question for reflection, 37
    Seen and the Unseen, 36
shaman, 190
shamanism, 190
Shinto, 83
Sphere of Protection, 231
spirit roads, 81
    exploring mysteries of spirit roads,
        81–83

    orientation, 81–83
    practical work, 83
    question for reflection, 83
    sacred paths and haunted routes,
        81–83
    surviving examples of, 82
spiritual traditions, ancient, 83
stone circles, 132
stories, 40, 103, 198
    enchantment of land, 103–105
    history, 104
    of industrial cultures, 104
    legend, 104
    myth, 104
    orientation, 103–105
    passing on secrets, 105
    power of, 103–105
    practical work, 105
    question for reflection, 105
stories of beginnings, 127
    archetypal power of beginnings,
        127–129
    creation myths, 127–129
    legends of beginnings, 127
    orientation, 127–129
    practical work, 129
    question for reflection, 129
stories of conventional wisdom, 143
    enchantment of wipes, 143–145
    orientation, 143–145
    practical work, 145
    pseudoskeptics, 144
    question for reflection, 145
    stories of disenchantment
        and, 143–145
    wipe, 144
stories of mysterious events, 135
    blurred boundaries, 135–137
    orientation, 135–137
    paranormal events, 136
    practical work, 137
    question for reflection, 137
    Terror That Comes in the Night,
        The, 136
    unraveling strange events, 135–137
stories of mysterious places, 131
    folklore studies, 132

myth, legend, and history, 131–133
orientation, 131–133
overlapping realms, 131–133
practical work, 133
question for reflection, 133
Rollright Stones, 132
stone circles, 132
stories of the future, 139
anticipating and interpreting future, 139–141
future in myth, legend, and popular culture, 139–141
narratives about future, 140
orientation, 139–141
practical work, 141
question for reflection, 141
UFO phenomenon, 140
Study Hill, 204, 205, 206. *See also* William Blackstone, legend of
Stukeley, Rev. William, 93
swamp lights, 186. *See also* earth lights

Terror That Comes in the Night, The, 136
trilithon, 70. *See also* megaliths

ufologists, 185
UFO phenomena and traditional wisdom, 189. *See also* unidentified flying objects
Flying Saucers: A Modern Myth of Things Seen in the Sky, 191
Jung, Carl, 191
orientation, 189–191
practical work, 191
question for reflection, 191
shaman, 190
shamanism, 190
UFO narratives in modern times, 190–191
UFOs. *See* unidentified flying objects
unconscious, collective, 116, 120, 121. *See also* archetype
unidentified flying objects (UFOs), 181. *See also* earth lights; UFO phenomena and traditional wisdom

as camouflage for tests, 182
fraud and deception, 182–183
narratives in modern times, 190–191
orientation, 181–183
phenomenon, 140, 154
practical work, 183
question for reflection, 183
Unseen, the, 8, 19–20. *See also* Seen and the Unseen
in landscape, 57
mapping out geography of, 74
rejection by industrial society, 136
sites, stories, and phenomena in, 197–199
tapping into the, 27–29
urban legends, 124

Watkins, Alfred, 77
Way of the Golden Section, The, 21, 24
Webb, Thomas, 218
Weber, Max, 11
Western meditation, 230
"wild Merlin". *See* Myrddin Wyllt
William Blackstone, legend of, 203
Blackstone and Yellow Sweeting apple, 205
conversation with Reverend William Blackstone, 206–207
directions to Study Hill, 207
discussion, 204–205
evidence, 203–204
investigation, 206–207
Johnny Appleseed, 205, 207
Myrddin Wyllt ("wild Merlin"), 205
pairing of man and bull, 204
Rhode Island, 203, 204
Study Hill, 204, 205, 206
"windows", 154, 194. *See also* clusters and connections
wipe, 144

Yeti, 170. *See also* hominids, mysterious

Milton Keynes UK
Ingram Content Group UK Ltd.
UKHW020749170924
448415UK00023BB/362